JULIAN SEDGWICK

GHOSTS OF SHANGHAI

Hodder
Children's
Books

a division of Hachette Children's Group

First published in Great Britain in 2015
by Hodder Children's Books

1

A Catalogue record for this book is available from the British Library

Typeset in Garamond by Avon DataSet Ltd,
Bidford-on-Avon, Warwickshire

ISBN 978 1 444 92390 2

The paper and board used in this book are made from wood from
responsible sources.

Hodder Children's Books
A division of Hachette Children's Group
Part of Hodder & Stoughton

Carmelite House, 50 Victoria Embankment,
London, EC4Y 0DZ

An Hachette UK Company
www.hachette.co.uk

For Jutta and Francis. With thanks.

Contents

A wise man once said: with our thoughts we make the world.

So imagine this . . .

第一章

THE RESTLESS

Amidst shadows and dragons and watchful, crumbling statues Ruby Harkner crouches in a corridor of White Cloud Temple, sweat prickling her paper-pale skin, heart bumping like mad – waiting to catch her first ghost.

She's terrified, excited, her eyes tight shut as she strains to hear the slightest sound that will tell her the fox spirit has returned. That it's time to spring the trap.

But there's not even a hint of it yet.

Half a long hot hour has passed since she and the gang took their positions, and her legs are stiff, fizzing with a million pins and needles. A slight doubt nags as she shifts her weight to ease them, a broken floorboard groaning beneath.

'Pssst, Ruby! That you?' A young girl's voice comes snaking out of the darkness, whispering street

1

Chinese. 'You are still there, aren't you?'

'Yesss. Of course I am,' she answers fluently. 'What is it *now*?'

'Can you hear anything?'

'Not yet. *Shhh—*'

Black thunder breaks low overhead and Ruby feels the old building shake. She opens her eyes and peers into the gloom of the main hall to check everyone is still in place. Good, Fei's kept to her task, squatting below the statue of the Jade Emperor, just where she's supposed to be. But when her voice comes again it's wavering.

'I dunno, Ruby. Maybe it's not coming?'

'It's coming,' Ruby says firmly, glancing down at her arms. 'I can feel it.'

Under her summer bloomed freckles the goosebumps are steadily rising. Even when she can't see the ghosts, she *knows* they are there. It's been this way ever since Tom died: she can sense them all around, pressing close, whispering cold words in the shell of her ear, weighing down her chest when she startles from sleep. Or banging the pipes in the dead of night, making her messy bob of blonde hair stand up on end.

She takes a deep breath. *Lai ba*, she mutters in Chinese. Come on, we're ready for you, fox.

The air is hot and damp, one of those evenings

in September when all the oxygen has been sucked from it, and the Ghost Society's first proper spirit hunt has reached a point of no return. The restless fox has been plaguing them for a week and enough is enough. It's time to reclaim their hideout in the ruined temple.

At least we have the Almanac to help us now, Ruby thinks. And the Almanac says to use your breathing to cope with fear, to count each breath slowly in and out to strengthen your *ch'i*, your vital life force. She grips the sky-blue spirit bottle in her sweaty hands, eyes raking the shadows.

Through the doorway she can still make out Fei tucked against one of the pillars in the main hall, acting as the bait, bravely slicing the bruised, over-ripe peaches that will draw the fox into the open. She's got real spirit, Fei, even though she's two years younger than the rest. Charlie, her brother, stands poised with a bucket of water that will quench the spirit's thirst, and help send it back to the Otherworld. The rest of the gang lurk somewhere beyond, waiting to attack.

But it's getting darker by the minute, and Charlie and Fei are nothing but deep shadows cut against the gloom, and that means the sun's setting, Ruby thinks. And that means I'll be in *big* trouble when I get home. Well, forget it now! Mother and Father can stew in their own juices. This is more important, more important by far, than their worries and black moods. This is real.

'Rubyyyyy?' Fei whispers again.

'Shhh. If you don't shut up it won't—'

But then she hears it. She hears the fox.

It's almost imperceptible. But the sound's real enough, whispering over the perpetual background hum of the city. A shuffling coming from the other corridor, as if someone – something – tired and hungry, is staggering through the building on its last legs. Ruby's heart bumps in her throat, like a plum stone has wedged itself there, throbbing.

'Can you hear *that*?' she hisses into the gloom.

'What?' Fei whispers back.

'That sound.'

'Think so. Shall I keep chopping?'

'Yes! Don't startle it.'

But the noise has stopped.

In the silence that follows, a ship moans out on the Huangpu River, a wounded, dying animal. Something flickers on the edge of her vision. Is it lightning, or the fox taking shape? That whole side of her body has gone *really* tingly, as if she's brushed an electric cable. Shivers snake over her skin.

Definitely here, Ruby thinks. *Mei wenti*. No problem.

She edges forward along the corridor, past the blackness of the old monks' cells and up two steps to the doorway of the main hall. The sweet aroma of peach clots the air, mingling with smoke from the sticks of incense they've had burning all afternoon.

'*The true hunter sees with the edge of their vision,*' the old Almanac declares. '*Aim your arrow away from the target to hit the bullseye.*'

Ruby looks up at the faded paint of the red and white dragons battling on the ceiling, and lets her eyes soften.

And she sees it: a vague, shimmery patch, like a cloud of dust particles, gathering, pulsing, taking shape in the corner of her vision. A head taller than a man, it's bending forward as it moves steadily, towards Fei. Ruby can hear it whispering, its voice a mess of Chinese syllables. But she can just make out the words.

'*Taozi! Taozi!* Peaches. Give me peachessss. Get out of my way! I *need* themmmm!'

It hesitates, shadowy paws raised, sniffing the incense, the peaches, the stink of the streets outside, the musty tang coming from the river, ten thousand smells that make up the stench of the great city. And licks its lips.

The excitement of the moment shunts Ruby's fear to one side.

A real *hu li jing!*

But she's not surprised the spirit has materialised. Not at all . . . It's just what she expects from a place like this, just what she expects from the city she's known all her life and that is as beautiful as it is weird and utterly strange.

And just what kind of city is it that conjures fox spirits out of nothing?

Imagine a place where worlds collide: a restless city, bursting at the seams, where neon light and luxury rub against disease and bewildering poverty. Where, in a few square miles, the citizens of a hundred nations are packed amongst two million natives, all looking for a better life, all trying to ignore or flee the vast country beyond gripped by fear and famine and war.

Imagine a place where you can be anything you want to be.

Where you can risk everything and make a fortune overnight – or disappear and lose your head. Where child workers dark factories, and the pleasure palaces never close. Where spies lurk outside department stores, and gangsters cruise the streets in long-nosed cars, carving through the business men and beggars like black sharks swimming teeming seas. A city poised on the edge between perfect ripeness and total ruin.

Where anything goes – and almost everything you can imagine does, and the air itself is charged with electricity.

Imagine a place where *nothing* is ever still, not even the dead in their graves.

Imagine the great city of Shanghai in September 1926.

第二章

THE WELL

The fox spirit gives a strangulated cry, and lunges forward.

'Now! Now!' Ruby propels herself into the main hall as hard as she can. Her elbow catches the pillar and something rips the skin there, burning, but there's no time to worry about that.

'Where is iiiit?' Fei shrieks, looking frantically over both shoulders, blue black plaits flying. 'Where the hell *is* it!?'

Lightning cuts the air, dazzling her for a second. Charlie is looking at Ruby now, the bucket gripped in his slim hands. 'What do I do?'

'Make sure it's in the incense smoke! Then chuck the water over it.'

'But I can't see *anything*!'

Ruby turns her head and sees that buzzy patch of

light again, growing, solidifying right in front of Fei. And you can smell a foxy stink filling the hall.

She points. 'It's *there*! At the peaches!'

Fei screams and drops the plate, backing away, stumbling and falling onto her back. The confusion seems to startle the spirit, because it fades again, slipping away into nothingness as Ruby runs towards it, pointing the neck of her spirit bottle like a blue gun.

'Now,' she shouts. 'The water!'

Charlie slops the bucket's contents through the incense – and the thunder detonates right overhead, shaking the building to its foundations, plaster and dust raining down. For a split second she sees the spirit clearly, as clear as midday sun: a tall figure dressed in rags, lush red tail beating the ground, its gaunt face trapped halfway between a man and a fox, silver fur around eyes that burn with desperation, drooling as it reaches towards Fei. It's powerful, much bigger than she imagined – and briefly her courage falters.

She steels herself and advances again, but the fox disappears into the smoky darkness.

'Andrei! Where *are* you?'

The Russian boy leaps clear over the altar, gripping the wooden spirit sword in his hands, the magical calligraphy they've daubed on the blade a blur. He looks at Ruby, eyes quick under his shaved head. '*Where* it is?'

Ruby glances at the floor. Are those wet footprints, moving towards her? Fear shunts the blood harder through her veins.

'There! Chop it!'

Andrei slices down where where she points and the blade thuds the rotten matting. He raises it again and starts hacking back and forwards through the smoke. With a shaking hand Ruby holds the bottle as close as she dares, waving it around and around in the incense.

'Into the bottle!' she shouts. 'Go home, old Mister Fox!'

Nothing seems to be happening. What if it doesn't go in? They'll just have enraged it . . .

But then the glass starts to feel colder in her hands. And weirdly heavy too, like when she held that block of ice at Fratelli's ice cream parlour in fast-numbing fingers. It's as if the bottle's filling to the brim with an icy liquid, almost too cold to handle.

Desperately she hangs on. It must be in now. She fumbles the cork down into the bottle's throat and holds it there, breathing hard, not daring to let go.

'We got it! I think we *got* it.'

Charlie peers at the bottle through his wire-rimmed

spectacles. 'I couldn't see anything.'

'For moment I see,' Andrei says, his Russian accent fumbling the Chinese. 'Horrible . . . *strashny*!'

Fei is sitting on the floor, hugging her knees, gazing at Ruby's hands and the glass fogged with condensation.

'And it's in there now? You're sure?'

'It's *really* cold. That's what the Almanac says, doesn't it, Yu?'

She looks up at the boy who's appeared in the main doorway, silhouetted against the dusk, the breeze rustling his Chinese gown.

Yu Lan nods. 'I've put binding characters on the label. It can't get out.'

They all gaze spellbound at the bottle, all except Charlie who turns and walks a few slow paces away towards the dusky courtyard.

Ruby senses his movement and turns to watch him go. In the sudden calm she can hear at first only her heart beating, but then the hum of the city returns as if someone's turning up the volume on the wireless. Street vendors are shouting on Honan Road and there's the shuddering of freight trains away to the north. A police whistle shrills the air close by.

Andrei glances in its direction. 'And now what we do?'

'Drop it down the well,' Ruby says. 'That should be deep enough.'

Charlie glances at Fei. 'Then we've *got* to go. No arguing, Sis.'

Ruby frowns. He doesn't seem very excited – not really – or impressed, she thinks, almost as if he'd rather be somewhere else. But what could be more important than *this*? In all our years and years as friends, this is the single most *thrilling* thing we've ever done.

'Charlie? Are you OK?' she asks.

'Just need to get back, that's all.' He shoots her one of his familiar crooked smiles, but it's gone almost before it registers and he tugs absently at the cuffs of his jacket to try and cover his wrists. The sleeves are just that bit too short now. He's shot up in the last year, she thinks. Sometimes it's like he thinks he's more grown up than the rest of us.

She glances away. Towards Nanking Road you can see neon in the gloom and a tram clanks past behind the temple wall, striking green sparks against the oncoming thunderclouds. The light really *has* faded, and it's much – MUCH – later than she thought. Bother. There'll be hell to pay when she gets back to the Mansions.

Yu Lan has closed the Almanac and ties the ribbon

round the faded covers before tucking it away in the hiding place behind the altar.

Heart still butterflying, Ruby crosses the courtyard to the well, holding the bottle carefully in her numbed hands. Mother always says she's cack-handed, an *accident waiting to happen*. Just like the girls at school who call her that and worse when they're not teasing her about her freckle-face. At Saint Joseph's, with the other British and American children, she feels clumsy and awkward all the time, tripping over her own feet, her words. Not like she has always felt in her 'Chinese World': alive, capable – skilful, even.

But even here she doesn't feel at ease these days.

The lightning flickers again, illuminating black and white photos of the dead on their forgotten gravestones. They stare unseeing from their glassed frames, and a shiver threatens to show in her hands. She grips tighter.

'Let's get it done.'

She holds the bottle over the drop.

Peering down, there's nothing to see but a darkness so thick you could slice it, just a soft breath of subterranean air coming up to brush her face.

'Rest peacefully mister fox spirit,' she says in her fluent Chinese, 'and don't bother us any more.' She checks again that the stopper is *really, really* tight, and then lets the bottle fall.

The well swallows it in one long, black gulp. Leaning over she strains to listen for the impact, but as usual, there's no splash, no breaking of glass, nothing to tell that it's hit the bottom – or give an idea what's down there.

Fei thrusts her hands into the pockets of her jacket. 'Auntie says it's a way into the Otherworld.'

'Don't be daft,' Charlie grunts. 'Dad says—'

'What does he know?' Fei snorts. She takes one of the bruised peaches from her pocket and lobs it into the well. 'Just in case anything's hungry down there.'

'We did it though,' Ruby says. 'That's the first proper one we've done. The book *works*!'

Her eyes are shining as she looks to each member of the gang. The stories Ruby devoured when she was small – the *Strange Tales* of hopping vampires, vengeful ghosts, shapeshifting foxes – are true after all.

'We defeated the *hu li jing* – and it was a really strong one. Maybe a Number Three ranking, even a Two. We'll have the place to ourselves again.'

'I hope so,' Charlie says quietly, doubt blunting his face. 'I really hope so.'

'What do you mean?'

'Nothing. We gotta get going, Sis.' He tugs Fei by the elbow. 'Dad needs us. *Zai jian*, see you tomorrow. Hopefully.'

'*Zai jian.*'

'You stay, Ruby?' Andrei asks, still clutching the spirit sword, his face hopeful. But Ruby's smile has disappeared with Charlie.

She shakes her head. 'Think I'll get back. Before it's dark.'

Ten minutes later she is trudging home under a grumbling sky, replaying the events of the afternoon. It really happened, she thinks, hands still sensing the cold of the spirit bottle. Now maybe *everything* will start to feel better, feel more like things used to be.

But Charlie's reaction has taken the edge off things . . .

The rain starts to fall, big heavy bullets of warm water that pock the dusty pavement. She glances up at the windows of their new apartment in Riverside Mansions, letting the rain spatter her face, delaying a moment longer. The building looks ridiculous, out of place, like a stupid wedding cake or something. Next to her looms the advertising hoarding for Soochow Sunshine Dairy. A happy Shanghailander family of four sit around on a picnic rug enjoying bright glasses of milk under the words: *Everyone's Happy and Healthy with Sunshine Milk! Healthy and sterilized!*

She pulls a face and eyes the windows of their eighth floor flat.

The elation of catching the fox is gone, replaced with the blackness of the well, the photographs on the tombstones blurred with condensation. She used to gaze at them with fascination, studying the faces of the departed intently for a clue as to what lay beyond. But they gave nothing away, and now she avoids them and the drops of water that gather and run behind the glass.

Tears of the dead, her Amah calls them.

Why doesn't Tom have a photo on *his* stone? Ruby asked once.

Because *we* don't do that, Mother said. The Chinese do, and we don't.

But—

No buts, Ruby. We're British. Not Chinese. Whether you like it or not. Now leave Thomas to rest in peace. And *remember* who you are.

She tries to block the image that comes so often, but it's too late, and fleetingly Ruby sees her brother laid in his coffin. Amah says if you don't weigh down the coffins here with enough lead shot, then – in the soft, silty earth beneath Shanghai – they start to move, drifting through the reclaimed marshy ground to Heaven knows where, voyaging on slow, dark currents underground.

Through the Otherworld.

The black moods of her parents aren't the only things troubling Ruby right now in Riverside Mansions. Even if the fox has been banished, who knows whether the other restless spirits will stay away, or return.

The thunder bangs again and Ruby pushes through the doors into the lobby, moving between the worlds.

第三章

THE VOICE FROM BEYOND

Every haunting begins somewhere and Ruby's started on a night six months ago when the paint still smelt wet on the walls of the new apartment and Tom wasn't long in his grave.

Winter was blowing snow flurries in from the troubled Interior of China, buffeting Riverside Mansions, and the luminous green hands of her alarm clock had just ticked to half past two.

She woke abruptly, rocketing from sleep, instantly aware that something *weird* was happening. She'd been having one of her recurring dreams, the one where she was flying across a vast landscape like the intrepid pilot she always longed to be, her eyes full of a shining, twisting river unfolding beneath. As she snapped awake the image seemed to linger a moment or two after waking – and then she heard the sound that

18

pushed it, and everything else, from her attention: a gasping coming from the ventilation grille on her bedroom wall.

It was a long, ragged sigh, like the beggar outside their old house on Bubbling Well Road who greeted her each morning with an exhausted wave and a horrific cough, struggling for breath . . .

But this sounded more animal than human. Or maybe something in between.

She sat up, every sense sharpening as the sound got louder and louder. Something was crawling slowly up the air conditioning shaft, getting closer by the second. A year or more ago and it would have excited her rather than scared, but not now, and Ruby's body went rigid with fear. The breathing sound was almost in the room, filling it – and then it stopped dead.

She could hear her pulse tapping in her ears, the clock on the bedside table cutting the sudden silence.

'Hello . . . ?' she whispered into the grainy darkness. '*Ni hao?*'

Above her then, she caught sight of movement. The frosted glass lampshade was starting to rock on its chain. Slowly at first and just an inch or two, but then in ever wider arcs, until it was scything through the air, as if someone was giving an extra shove at the top of each swing.

Still dreaming?

She pinched her arm, felt the nip of pain, and gazed back wide-eyed at the swaying lamp. Any harder and the glass would smash against the ceiling. Ruby was about to stand up, gathering courage to reach out and grab it with her trembling fingers, when the swing seemed to lose energy. At that precise moment there was a bang from the ventilation shaft, so loud that it sounded like a gunboat shell exploding.

And then nothing more.

Pale blue eyes wide, she sat up the rest of the night, watching the clock's hands drag, arguing with herself about possible causes, hoping that in the morning her parents would mention an earth tremor to explain that loud thump.

But they didn't.

And she already knew what it was: the new apartment block was haunted, just like in the stories Amah had told her since she was young: shapeshifting women who were monsters in disguise, sad-eyed ghost dogs, thin banshees who sat on your chest and sucked your vital *ch'i* from your body.

As she rides up now in the lift, the graze on her elbow stinging, she shivers to remember those first few days. How overwhelmed she felt, how afraid of what others might say, how alone. I should have told people sooner, she thinks. Just didn't want to make a fool of myself. In front of Charlie. He always listens carefully to whatever anyone has to say – no matter who they are – chewing things over for a long moment, then giving a fair opinion. Any other secret she would have shared immediately, but not this. He would have dismissed it out of hand – and so she waited for more, keeping it to herself.

She didn't have long to wait.

Objects seemed to move in her bedroom when she wasn't there. Or disappeared entirely, like Tom's broken clockwork monkey with its clashing cymbals that she still kept on her dressing table. One morning it was there and the next it was gone. Mother denied throwing the *horrid old thing* away, but then gave her an odd look that unnerved even more. Two nights later Ruby thought she heard the monkey's whirring chatter and clash, close by but muffled, as if sealed in a cupboard or tucked under a blanket. But no matter how hard she looked there was no sign.

Then there was the book, she thinks, the illustrated *Strange Tales*. It did that weird thing where it flipped into the air by itself. There was a flurry of pages like a bird startling and it plummeted to the ground where it lay, spine broken and pages splayed, her skin bumping as she tried to summon the courage to pick it back up.

21

Worse followed. As the weeks lengthened, she had the recurring sensation that someone, something, was standing right behind her, as if about to tap her on the shoulder or grab hold. Ruby would count to three, and spin round to confront nothing but empty air, or her own confused face staring back from the antique mirror in the hall, blinking in alarm.

Night after night, she did her best to calm the fears. Nothing can hurt me, she repeated to herself. *Mei wenti.* Nothing ever scares you, Ruby, Tom always used to say admiringly. But it did now, and the more she pushed it away the stronger it became. The girl who once raced the Chinese streets eager for life and adventure started to fade into memory.

And then the day things came to a head: she was stirring one of Amah's suspicious attempts at Mulligatawny soup, when the old lady's windchimes started to move by themselves. The stained-glass window was shut, there wasn't a trace of breeze inside or out, but even so the bells started to jingle and shake like mad. Rooted to the spot, Ruby watched as they jerked violently, the dragons carved on each silver bell dancing, the ringing echoing back off the kitchen walls. The temperature plummeted, as if someone had opened the door to their new refrigerator and stood her right inside – and her last drop of courage was gone.

'Amah!' she called in terror, dropping the ladle with a clatter to the tiled floor. 'Amah!!'

The old family servant was there in a moment, brown paper face scrunched in concern.

'What under Heaven is that racket—'

Her own colour drained from her as the bells went on jangling. Slowly Amah reached for Ruby's hand, and together they watched in silence until at last the chimes trembled to a stop.

'What is it, Amah?' Ruby whispered.

'We have a restless spirit,' the old lady said quietly. 'I told you they should never have built on this ground. But don't worry. *Most* spirits and foxes don't hurt people. I'll go to ask the *sifu* at New Moon Temple what we should do.'

'What if *he* can't help?'

'Always help when you need it somewhere. Don't worry, Ruby – did I ever tell you about when I was little and an old fox cast a spell on our village? He was dressed up as a young man, but really it was just a skin he pulled on as he went about his foxy business of seducing young women and luring them to his den in the hills . . .' And off she went, spinning a familiar story into Ruby's ears. Once she would have lapped it up, and believed a lot of it too, but now Amah's story felt too close to home. All too real.

23

As August crushed Shanghai with heat and the hauntings got more and more frequent, fear left its mark on Ruby's skin, drawing rings under her eyes, prickling her flesh constantly, transforming her from a girl who once knew no fear at all, to one held almost permanently in its grip. And at last the effort to keep her secrets from the others became too much too bear.

In their den at White Cloud, Charlie, Fei and Andrei listened intently as she poured out her story about the chimes, the breathing, the monkey.

No one spoke at first as she looked eagerly from face to face.

'You do believe me, don't you?'

Charlie puffed out his cheeks. '*Bu zhi dao*. Dunno—'

Fei's eyes had opened wide as saucers and she dug her elbow into Charlie's ribs. 'But of course! Everyone knows this part of town is rotten with foxes.'

'I was here other night,' Andrei said, leaning forward eagerly, meaty hands gripping his knees. 'We got nowhere to sleep after Mama lose job. I can't stay where she staying . . . And I think I *hear* something. There were noises back in old rooms. When I go to look there is something in the corner of one, but when I shout, it just seem to disappear.'

'Why didn't you say?' Charlie sniffed.

'Because nobody believe me. Then later I hear this

24

weird howl.' He tipped his head back and moaned a long falling note that should have been funny but somehow unsettled them all, even Charlie shifting uncomfortably. Above, the shadowy statue of the Jade Emperor stared down from under his fierce, heavy eyebrows.

'You see, Charlie?' Ruby said anxiously, trying to gauge his reaction.

'It was probably just a stray dog.'

'Then what about that thing we saw by Soochow Creek. That hopping vampire,' Fei protested. 'You nearly wet yourself.'

Charlie groaned. 'We were *really* little then. Dad says—'

'But it was real!' Ruby implored. 'You should have *seen* those wind chimes.'

The conversation died to awkward silence, leaving Ruby frustrated, worried Charlie thought she was acting like a little kid.

But surely now he believes her after that encounter with the fox?

She hesitates and wipes a fresh ooze of blood from her arm. In the corridor her own footsteps bounce back off the walls, and she hurries, glancing over her shoulder, the distant thunder muffled but ominous. By the time

Ruby's through their front door, the full weight of the storm is battering Riverside Mansions. The mirror in the hall reflects the sitting room windows beyond, lightning whiting out the sky.

'Where the blazes have you been?' Father snaps from behind his paper, making her jump. 'It's way past your curfew and it's filthy out.'

'I was with the Tangs,' she says, longing to tell someone about the fox, but there's no point with Dad. He always declares he has no time for *superstitious bilge*. Better not to make matters worse. 'I'm sorry—'

'You need to wake up, Ruby. Pay attention to the real world.' He shakes the paper, trying to jar the words there into better sense.

'But I *am* paying attention—'

'You do NOT need *me* to tell you what your mother has been through . . .' he adds, biting off his own words.

'No,' she murmurs. Once he would have smiled to see her having fun, *running wild*, but that seems like another world now, the one where he would ruffle her hair and call her *Shanghai Ruby*. These days he's always so preoccupied with work, with Mother. 'Sorry.'

'If you only knew what she's been going through.'

But what about me? Ruby thinks. What about what *I've* been through?

Father prods the headline on the front of the paper, holds it out for her to see. 'You need to listen to us about where and when you go places. Understand?'

In bold letters the North China Daily News declares: COMMUNISTS AGITATING IN CITY. DEATHS REPORTED.

Best not be too stubborn, she thinks. Show some interest. 'Communists? Are they like the Nationalists?'

'Pfff. A bit – but worse. They don't want the likes of us here.'

'Will there be a revolution? Like in Russia?'

'God, no. And we'll be fine. International Settlement's safe as houses.'

'They're piling sandbags at the checkpoints, and there's tanks on the Bund by the river.'

'Just goes to show how safe we are. But you need to stick in the Settlement for now, and the French Concession. Keep out of the Old City—'

'But Nantao's more fun.'

'No blasted "buts", Ruby,' Father growls, trying to make his damaged leg comfortable. 'They're for goats. Nantao is under that crackpot of a warlord and those Green Hand thugs are really running the show there—'

Mother comes in, hands clasped in front of her. She sees Ruby and takes a sharp gasp of air.

'I've been worried sick, Ruby—' Her gaze falls on the bloodied elbow.

'*What* have you done to yourself?'

'Nothing, I—'

'Amah?' Mother calls, voice jagged. 'Amah! Fetch Germolene and some hot water! Ruby's gone and cut herself the *stupid* girl.'

Amah bustles in as fast as she can on her tiny, bound feet. 'Now then, Miss Ruby, we'll get this cleaned up in no time,' she clucks away in Shanghai dialect.

'English, Amah!' Mother snaps. 'Speak English, or Pidgin at least so I can understand. Savvy?'

Amah nods. 'Savvy.'

'And tell your nephew and niece not to be so rough.'

'No problem, Missee Harkner.'

'Amah!' Ruby whispers hurriedly in Chinese, unable to contain herself. 'We did it. We got the fox!'

'English!' Father pleads. 'So we can all join in.'

Amah winks, and leads her away past the mirror to the bathroom, whispering in dialect. 'Then you've done better than that hopeless *sifu* at the joss house. The only spirit he understood came in a bottle.'

'It worked,' Ruby whispers back, and Amah listens intently to the story of the cleansing of the fox spirit, applauding quietly.

'I've always said it, Ruby. You've got the knack.

And you one of them foreign devils!'

Ruby frowns. 'I was born here, Amah. I'm *not* a foreigner.'

Later, elbow cleaned and bandaged, she goes to stand by the window. The only thing she really likes about the new place is how it makes her feel she's hovering over the city. Like that Taoist trick of leaving your body and floating high overhead to view the world like an eagle.

Her gaze roves across the skyline. Beyond the waste ground, what she and the others have always called 'the Wilderness', she can see the lights of the Plum Blossom Dance Hall and the Great World Amusement Palace, sweet neon colours running in the rain: raspberry, lemon, white. The traffic's still thickening the main artery of Nanking Road and below her, on the wide, windswept stretch of river, the warships of America, Japan, Britain and France are moored bow to stern, flags shivering at mastheads. Even in this weather sampans and junks are jostling on the water. On the far bank chimneys chug grey-white smoke above Pudong, factory nightshifts beginning.

She thinks of her friends, the members of the Ghost Society.

Blood sisters and brothers: Andrei, all heart and

fists, probably trying to find somewhere to bed down for the night, hungry as ever; rich Yu Lan, the newest member of the gang, being pampered inside his father's mansion. She thinks of Charlie and Fei snug in their alleyway house, the place always filled with their father's sharp humour as he emerges from his writing room to greet visitors, his faced dobbed with ink. She wishes she was there now – eating buns, drinking cups of steaming tea, listening to the gossip or Fei telling a funny story, pulling ridiculous faces as she boasts of how she'll be a movie star one day. And Charlie bursting into laughter . . . or leaning forward in earnest talk with visitors to the house, as they discuss China and its problems.

Anywhere but this antiseptic apartment block that wants to pretend China doesn't really exist. She wishes she was with Charlie. That they had more time together—

Her elbow's throbbing again.

What if something's got in there? Some stupid germ. Forget it, she thinks. I'm protected now, right? But is the talisman Yu drew for me just for foxes and ghosts or does it include germs and diseases? They're all threats, aren't they? It should work for illness too then . . .

She pulls the carefully folded and refolded piece of

yellow paper from her pocket and studies it intently. A complex kind of old Chinese character, forty-eight strokes and squiggles of the brush. You mustn't miss a single one and you need to do it in the right order, Yu Lan said, or it won't work. She refolds the talisman and pushes it under her pillow.

According to the Almanac, *Clouds grind down mountains. Water rusts the sword. This talisman repels all evil.*

The yellow paper crackles reassuringly as she puts her head down. Nothing weird has happened in the flat since Yu traced it out, just that familiar fragment of a dream now and then on the edge of sleep, the river snaking towards a vast horizon.

I'm protected, she thinks as she drifts down towards the water. *Mei wenti*

Her sleep is so deep that half an hour later she doesn't hear gunfire breaking against the night just a few streets away. So secure that she doesn't catch a word of the stop-start argument in the corridor later as her parents go to bed.

'The girl's fine,' Father grunts. 'Stop worrying for Heaven's sake, Stella.'

'We should go back to Doctor Sprick. Remember the *awful* night terrors she had when she was small. And that heartbeat still isn't—'

'Man's a quack. Take a sleeping pill or two and get some rest. Please.'

'She's paler than normal. If they weren't related to Amah I'd stop her running with those Tang children. Have you *seen* how that boy looks at her sometimes?'

'They're just kids. But it might be best *if* she doesn't spend so much time with them.'

'Why?'

'Something brewing. One or two people about to get their fingers burnt,' Father rumbles. 'Or chopped right off. Maybe it's time we started thinking about sending her home. All of us going even. It might be safer.'

He bumps the door shut as the last of the gunfire echoes down the Huangpu, towards the Yangtze River and into the huge continent beyond.

Next morning the storm has gone. Rickshaws swish the damp roads, and Shanghai smells almost fresh, the usual stench from the river and the honey-carts that slop raw sewage to distant fields banished. At least for an hour or so.

A few bright clouds are pinned to the blue dome above and the day lifts in front of her like when she was younger and everything was easy, when she and Tom explored the outskirts of the sprawling city and watched puppet plays about King Monkey and his expulsion from Heaven, or marvelled at fire eaters and contortionists.

As she strides towards the temple she whistles a scrap of Chinese folk song. Still a few days to the start of school and no one to call her *toad face* or *beetroot Ruby*. And no bad dreams last night, she thinks. No bumps in the night. The talisman is working, just like the Almanac promised.

第四章

THE GHOST HUNTER'S MANUAL

The book appeared the very day after she told about the ghosts. As if unseen forces had conjured it straight into Ruby's hands at just the right moment.

Ruby and the Tangs were rummaging at the back of Mister Uchiyama's bookshop, hunting for an illustrated copy of *Outlaws of the Marshes*. The Japanese bookseller always welcomed everyone, from local writers to impoverished 'White' Russians looking to sell books and keep hunger at bay. Ruby had loved it ever since Father took her there to ask about a set of astronomy magazines, its three rooms crammed with books in Chinese, English, French, Russian, and she would wile away the afternoon reading in a corner as the sun moved across the dusty windows.

Ruby picked her way between tottering stacks, past two Chinese men in western suits locked in heated, whispered debate. One of them was tall, lean like a greyhound, the other thick round the middle and crammed tight into his suit. They were bent over some kind of street map, but broke off to glance at Ruby as she went by. The taller one raised his hat, stepping aside to let her past, sun picking out its emerald green lining. Focussed on her hunt, Ruby paid them little attention . . .

It was Charlie who wanted a new copy of the stories of the heroic robbers of the 'Water Margin', but Ruby was keen to be the one to find it for him. As ever there seemed no order to Uchiyama's shop: a leather-bound Dickens was sandwiched between a fiery Russian pamphlet and a book of 'Callisthenics for Young Ladies'. Irritated for once by the chaos, Ruby turned and knocked another stack – sending books crashing to the ground – and revealed a curious, battered volume lying on the floorboards.

The book was bound in faded green and lay there in a pool of sunshine, as if spotlit for attention. The title stamped vertically in smudgy Chinese was hard to read, but she recognized a couple of the characters as saying 'OTHER WORLD'. Ruby hesitated, then reached out and felt the linen of the cover. It was strangely cold to the touch, and she fancied she felt a small tingle travel up her fingers and arm. She took a breath then picked it up and carried it in both hands to Uchiyama's cluttered desk.

The bookseller peered over his half-moon spectacles.

'Found it then?'

'No. But what's this?'

Uchiyama squinted at the characters.

'Main title: *Almanac of the Other World*.' He frowned. 'Subtitle: *Methods for Green Frontier*. Don't remember getting that one in – maybe it was the previous owner's stock.'

The others were gathering around as he undid the ribbon and flicked the blotched pages. As he turned them, the paper crackled and – peering over his shoulder – Ruby's excitement mounted. She glimpsed complicated diagrams, woodcuts of strange looking creatures, and weird Chinese characters sprawling across the page. The shivers were working her skin all over now.

'What is it?'

'This,' Uchiyama said, tapping a page, 'is old Taoist handbook for banishing ghosts and things like that. Maybe from middle of Ching dynasty? "*Other World*" is place where the spirits live. "*Green Frontier*" is where you cross over . . .'

Ruby's eyes popped wide. Just like Amah had said – something or someone turning up to help.

'Woah!' Fei's mouth made a perfect 'O' as she stared at the book. 'Is it real? It must be worth a lot!'

Uchiyama laughed, turning the book in his hands. 'It's in bad condition. No real use—'

'I want to buy it,' Ruby said, fishing in the pocket of her dress for some silver taels. 'How much?'

The bookseller sighed. 'I really couldn't—'

'But why *not*?'

'I'd be robbing you if I asked more than a dollar.'

'But it must be worth tons more than that.'

Uchiyama shook his head.

Ruby eagerly handed him a small silver coin and the bookseller waved her away, turning to the two men burrowing through the chest, the smile dropping from his long face. 'Now, gentlemen. A street map, you say? But older?'

Ruby's eyes were fixed on the book in her hands and she led the others excitedly to the back of the shop.

'I told you I don't believe in ghosts,' Charlie said. 'It's just superstition—'

Fei shook her head impatiently, jinking her plaits. 'Fathead. You should've listened properly to Auntie and what she's seen.'

Ruby looked at Charlie, anxious not to seem foolish again. 'I can't read characters well enough,' she said, pushing what she felt was her most winning smile across her face. 'I need *your* help to read it.'

Charlie gazed at the book, then shrugged his shoulders. 'I'll take a look for you, but—'

'Thank you,' she said, relief flooding through her, resisting the urge to give him a quick, shy hug.

Later that afternoon at White Cloud, Charlie peered at the book, biting his lip for what seemed like an age, as Ruby paced the shaky veranda.

'Well?' she said at last.

'It's classical style . . . I dunno. Waste of time anyway.'

'Maybe we need someone who can read *properly*,' Fei said, pulling a face.

'What about that rich kid, Yu Lan. The one on Rue du Consulat?' Andrei asked. 'My brother used to work as a guard for his old man when we first arrive. He has tutors. Old scholars.'

'But he's not one of us,' Fei protested.

'We don't need his sort,' Charlie added. 'Compradors like him are just getting rich off everyone else's misery—'

'Oh, let's try,' Ruby cut in. 'Can you get him, Andrei?'

'Sure. I see him at Great World sometimes. We

both go to see Electric Girl dance and shoot sparks from her fingers . . .'

If Andrei said he would do something you could normally rely on him to do it, and the next day Yu Lan duly appeared. Chubby, his hair tucked under a silk cap and wearing a midnight blue gown, he looked every inch the son of a wealthy trader. Maybe a bit too full of himself, Ruby thought, as Yu's eyes flicked around the temple with a mixture of curiosity and distaste. Something about his face I don't quite trust – but as long as we're careful, and he can read the book for me.

'At your service,' Yu said in English.

It didn't sound like he meant it. But when Ruby brought out her most polite Chinese, and then produced the Almanac, the look of disdain slipped from his face.

'Let me have it,' he said, sweeping the cap from his head, hair springing up as if shot with static. Within ten minutes he was engrossed, his eyes racing down each page. 'It's classical Chinese. Some of the characters are very old versions . . . *amazing* stuff!'

'Read it to me,' Ruby said. 'Don't miss anything out.'

As the afternoon heat boiled Yu deciphered the characters, spelling out possible meanings, while Ruby craned over his shoulder trying to make sense of the diagrams. Bit by bit, the book yielded descriptions of '*Correct Methods for Classifying Foxes*', for '*Spirit Boxing and Cultivating Ch'i*'.

'*The one true secret,*' Chapter One declared, '*is to pay attention and know your enemy.*' It listed possible foes: the Foxes, graded Four to One (the most serious and dangerous); Hopping Vampires with rigid limbs; Vengeful Ghosts capable of attacking the living; Poltergeists. '*The more serious matter of Revenants to be covered in a later chapter*' the Almanac promised, but the mysterious figure of the Silver Fox '*cannot be covered here, and must remain for those who deeply know the Way.*'

The book seemed to be working a kind of magic on Charlie too, because, by the end of the day, he was keen to keep reading, searching out Taoist martial arts' exercises, swishing hands around his head and checking the Almanac again to see if he was doing it right.

Puffing hard, he threw a glance at Yu. 'We've got to strengthen ourselves. Shanghai's always been too soft. That's why we're in a mess now.'

Ruby smiled.

By the time the sun was setting red in the West they had agreed to form the Shanghai Ghost Society. The old club papers – from when they called themselves the Outlaws – were dug up from their hiding place. Ruby changed the title at the top, and asked Yu to dab a drop of his blood where the others had signed and then smudged their own bloody thumbprints what seemed a half a lifetime ago. Her pale eyes lingered a moment on Tom's signature and the rusty splodge next to it. How much he'd have enjoyed this, she thought—

'Hey Ruby,' Fei said, jabbing excitedly at a diagram in the Almanac. 'Yu reckons this talisman will help. As long as you keep it close nothing will be able to hurt you.'

Under Fei's quivering index finger a convoluted Chinese character glowed like a maze in the evening light.

第五章

MOONFACE

A street short of the temple, Ruby waits as the traffic grinds past.

A Sikh policeman in a red turban whistles to keep order as a long-nosed car purrs by, the inverted 'V's on its radiator snarled like a shark's mouth. On either side, perched on the running boards, two tough, brutally thin Chinese men scan the crowded street with piercing eyes. One of them has his hand tucked under his jacket, the other shouting at a wayward rickshaw man to keep clear. As he raises his hand a flash of ink burns emerald on his palm and in the car's darkened interior a bulky figure is just visible as shadow.

Part of the Green Hand, she thinks with distaste.

Maybe that's the infamous Moonface himself on the back seat. He pretends to be a respectable businessmen, but everyone knows he's just a ruthless gangster. You see him in the paper every week with his big pock-marked face, always wearing that coat with the fur collar whatever the weather. The rumour goes that years ago in his home village he drowned his mother in a barrel of rice wine – and never looked back. His men rule the underworld in Shanghai, Charlie says. Vermin, best avoided. It's all opium and smuggling and much worse. They'll kill someone even if they *think* you said something bad about them. Lower ranking members have that green mark on their palms, the more important are supposed to have an emerald lining to their Trilby hats.

With a grimace, she watches the car cruise away towards Nanking Road. The glimpse of the Green Hand, and thinking about Charlie has punctured her mood. Last night should have been our greatest moment so far, she thinks, and yet, he was uninterested at the end.

For Ruby it's *his* reaction that matters most.

At White Cloud, Fei, Andrei and Yu are sitting in a block of sunshine on the front steps, a stick of incense jammed in the matting next to them, sending smoke coiling around their heads. The Almanac lies open.

Their heads whip around as one when they hear Ruby's footsteps approaching.

'Oh, it's you,' Fei says, a shadow chasing from her face.

'Who did you think it was?'

'Thought maybe it was the fox again,' Andrei grunts.

'Why? We got rid of it.' Ruby looks at each of them in turn. 'You shouldn't start without us all being here.'

Fei shakes her head, plaits twitching. 'We haven't really. Andrei heard something again and we're just checking—'

'We're supposed to work all together,' Ruby says. 'And *where's* Charlie?'

Fei shrugs. 'He's helping Dad with something. But he'll be here soon, *if* he can. Wouldn't count on it though. Not if you'd seen Dad's face.'

Ruby's heart sinks. That proves it doesn't it? Charlie's really not interested. She rubs at the wound scabbing her elbow. 'So when did you lot get here?'

'Half an hour ago,' Fei says. 'But Andrei had to spend the night.'

The Russian boy picks at the matting, his face colouring in embarrassment. 'I got chucked out of shelter,' he mutters. 'No choice.'

'And? You heard something again?'

Andrei screws up his face, fishing for the words. She

44

senses his frustration: that gap between what he wants to say and what his grasp of the language allows him.

He points at the ground. 'Like far away, but down there.'

Ruby looks out at the courtyard, the graves huddled beyond the well. Something's wrong again – her skin feels like it's trickling with cold water.

Andrei looks up. 'But another thing. There's a clairvoyant on Red Flower Street, friend of family. She told Mama there's a bad thing coming. She called it a 'Terror'. I'm trying to get Yu to see in book about that.'

Yu Lan shakes his head. 'Who trusts a foreign fortune teller?'

'Maybe it's like one of those revenants in the Almanac,' Ruby says. 'We should wait for Charlie—'

There's a sound behind them, deep in the temple, a soft, but distinct thump chopping her words short. Ruby freezes, listening hard. Nothing else follows for a good half a minute but then a series of rapid blows rattles the old roof tiles. And then silence again.

'What the hell was THAT?' Fei whispers.

'Sounds like it's coming from the monks' corridor,' Ruby says.

'Can't be a fox in broad daylight, though, can it?' Yu Lan mutters.

'In the *Strange Tales* they're always shapeshifting,' Ruby whispers. 'Then they seem just like normal people right? They could walk down the street at midday, Amah says, and you wouldn't even guess unless you knew how to look. You have to spot their fuzzy edges, otherwise you wouldn't know—'

Fei tugs her sleeve. 'What do we do?'

'Go and look of course,' Ruby mutters, trying to look braver than she feels, the goosebumps rising on her skin like drops of water on cold glass.

She leads the others back through the hall, down the two steps between peeling vermillion pillars, into the corridor. Her chest feels constricted as she and the others approach the doorway to the first cell. The scraps of sun falling through the broken shutters don't reach far into the room and the rest is blackness.

'Who's got matches?'

'Me,' Andrei says. 'I go first. Protect you.'

She's glad of that – but then it's as if the Ruby of old is pushing her way back, barging past the girl who's been held by fear this last year. 'No. I'll go first,' she says quickly.

Andrei shrugs, pulls a box of Phoenix matches from his pocket and strikes one on the door frame. The sulphur splutters, sending light dancing into the room.

She can see nothing unusual, just the remains of the old sleeping platform slowly crumbling to dust. They all listen hard until the match fizzes out, and Ruby beckons them on.

'Next one.'

Again a match flares in Andrei's thick fingers – but again this cell, apart from the broken chest that's been there ever since they first explored the temple, is empty.

'I can smell something,' Fei says, sniffing the air. 'Smoke.'

'That's just the match,' Yu hisses.

'No. Tobacco!'

Ruby grabs the matchbox and stalks into the third, even darker chamber, striking light as she goes – and stops still on the threshold. Three planks are resting on a couple of old crates, making a kind of bench. And sitting on those is a battered backpack and a bedroll. The fug of smoke is stronger here and a small stove sits to one side, a dented kettle perched on top.

'How long's that been there?' Fei says. 'Must be some beggar.'

'Didn't see it yesterday,' Ruby whispers.

Yu pulls a face. 'Let's just chuck his stuff out on the road.'

'No,' Andrei says. 'That would be bad.'

Ruby lifts her head, listening hard. 'Hello? Anyone here? We're friends.'

Nothing in reply, but the faint stirring of the breeze, the rustling of bamboo in the courtyard outside. Is that a sound above them? Andrei glances up.

'Rats? I saw huge black one last night.'

Ruby frowns. It sounds more like water running in a gutter – or someone chuckling quietly. The rippling on her skin fizzes even harder, and then the match flame stings her fingertips. She drops both it and the box, and everything goes dark. As she bends to scrabble blindly for it with her fingertips, she hears a familiar voice.

'Feiiii! Ruuuuubyyyy!'

Charlie! At last.

It's a really good sign if he's come after all – even though Mister Tang needed him for something urgent. He does care about the Society, she thinks. Cares about me . . .

She hurries back through the building, a smile lifting her anxiety. 'There you are! I was worried sick you weren't coming—'

Charlie's standing on the veranda, slim shoulders hunched in a shallow question mark. One look at his face tells her something's wrong, and her own spirits sink as she guesses what's coming.

'Change of plans. Sorry.'

'What do you *mean*?' she stammers.

'We've got to do something for Dad,' Charlie says, glancing away just like last night, his mind already clearly somewhere else. 'BOTH of us, Sis.'

Ruby seeks out Charlie's eyes. 'Couldn't you stay a bit? Some tramp's put his stuff back there and we've just heard some weird noises—'

Charlie shakes his head. 'Haven't got time for this.'

He glances back at Ruby and flashes an apologetic smile. 'Not today anyway.'

'Well, why don't I – why don't we all – come with you?' she says quickly. Surely the day, the precious time with Charlie can't slip that quickly from grasp? But his face is tightening again.

'It's not good for you to be in that part of the city. Not now.'

'But I'm not like the other foreign devils—'

'No, Ruby!' Charlie's voice whips back with a force that shocks her. 'It's not safe. The old city's really dangerous for foreigners.'

'But there's *loads* of missionaries in Nantao.'

'Yeah, but they're all barking mad.'

Ruby opens her mouth to argue back, but seeing the look on his face, she shuts it tight again. It's unusual for him to be that forceful, that abrupt. He'll normally reason things out, or soften an argument with a joke.

'We'll have to meet tomorrow.'

'But what about what we just heard?'

'They're driving piles for the new hotel on the corner,' Charlie says. 'Probably that. Come on, Fei.'

Without another word, without even a backward glance, he sets off at a brisk trot, past the well, past the graveyard, out of sight, his little sister hurrying to follow.

第六章

NO CHOW

Back out on the streets, alone, Ruby drifts with the crowd. Quickly her irritation has given way to anxiety, disturbed by the skittery look in Charlie's dark eyes. What could be so important as to drag the Tangs away like that? she thinks. And why didn't Fei put up more of a fight? She took one glance into Charlie's face and then just gave in. That's not like her at all.

She passes a limbless beggar on his cart and absently clatters a coin in the cup in front of him. Mother says not to, but every good deed will be reported to the Jade Emperor next month and it makes her feel good to help. And the beggar smiles so he's feeling better too. So where's the harm?

A brass band from some British regiment comes thumping past, parting the crowds, sun bright on instruments and buttons. Drilling down the middle of the street as if they damn well own the place! A soldier winks at her, but she looks the other way. I'm not one of you, she thinks crossly. Don't include me.

And as she turns her head she catches sight of the Tangs again.

They're standing at the street corner, facing each other, having a brief but intense argument. Charlie's ticking off a list on his fingers as he lectures his younger sister. She shakes her head once, but he just grabs her by the arm and then *drags* her on past the building works.

Now, that's *even weirder*. Charlie never pushes or pulls Fei around, not even when the younger girl lashes out. What on *earth's* going on? Come to think of it, this isn't the first time in the last few weeks that Charlie and Fei have changed plans at the last moment.

But it's no use pressing to find out what's causing that anxiety in Charlie's eyes. The harder you press the more he digs in his heels – like the other day when she'd bumped into them near their alleyway house, and found Fei crying her eyes out. Charlie acted like there was nothing wrong.

'Forget it. She's just being a baby.'

But Fei *never* cries. Never. It's a fierce point of honour with her.

There and then, Ruby decides to follow them, 'Shanghai Ruby' taking firm charge again with her courage and bounding curiosity.

Briefly, it crosses her mind she's breaking their blood oath – the fourth rule on the club papers: *each and every member will respect and trust the other members.* I shouldn't be spying on them, she thinks. But they shouldn't be keeping secrets from the rest of us. From *me*.

Rounding the corner she sees the Tangs veering across the road towards a noodle seller setting up his stall. He hasn't even lit his fire yet – and it's far too early for lunch, so what do they want with him? Ruby checks her pace, tucking into the shadows in case Charlie and Fei look round. The Almanac says, *if you don't want to be seen, then blank your mind. Think of not thinking until your mind is like a sky with no clouds. You will as good as disappear . . .* But how on earth do you do that?

The noodle seller nods at the Tangs as if he knows them, though Ruby's never seen the man before round here. He glances up and down the street once – twice – and then reaches under his stall to produce a package. Ruby only sees it for a moment, something about the size of a large book wrapped in newsprint, before Charlie swipes the thing and stows it under his faded blue jacket. Without another word or glance back, he and Fei set off at a dog trot towards the checkpoint on Avenue des Deux Republiques.

What's going on?

Ruby hustles through the crowds to follow. A honey cart comes rattling down the street, blocking her view, the stink from its cargo clearing the road. She nips round, holding a hand over her mouth, and is surprised to find the noodle seller already packing his stall away, not one meal prepared.

'*No chow,*' he hisses in Pidgin, waving her away. '*Savvy?*'

'*No wantee chow,*' Ruby says, annoyed, baffled, and turns to see the Tangs hurrying under the fluttering banners, two figures dwarfed by the enormous Chinese characters snapping overhead advertising *No. 1 Fish Sauce, North China Famine Relief, Lucky Lottery.*

If they're in some kind of trouble I need to know, she thinks, struggling to keep the Tangs in sight as she walks quickly after them. Maybe I can help. For a fleeting moment she imagines Charlie thanking her, throwing his arms around her in gratitude . . . Then shakes it away. Not now, too much else to think about.

The checkpoint between the International Settlement and the Chinese City is approaching. If they go through it, then I should stop, Ruby thinks, remembering Dad's warning. He's still pretty relaxed about where I go – at least compared to Mother. Almost like he doesn't care some days. But last night he obviously meant it.

Charlie and Fei could still turn for the French Park, somewhere up there in the Concession would be fine. But no, straight and true, the Tangs are marching towards the clutter of sandbags and barbed wire that mark the crossing, merging with the crowd.

If I don't go too far in, she mutters to herself, then nothing really awful can happen to me can it? Not in broad daylight. I'm protected against foxes and stuff, and as for the rest, I know what I'm doing.

Mei wenti. No problem.

She shoves forward into the throng waiting to cross into the Chinese City. Two men block her view for a moment, Chinese in suits, their black hats pulled down firmly on their heads. The chubbier one glances over his shoulder, eyes scouring the crowd behind. Something familiar about him, Ruby thinks vaguely, but in the helter skelter of the moment she can't place him . . .

. . . and then drops the thought as a policeman

blows his whistle, the checkpoint opens and the Tangs, the black suited men, Ruby and the rest of the waiting crowd are sucked through and into China proper.

第七章

THE DOG

The checkpoint is intimidating.

Roughly lashed poles support tangles of razor wire that shimmer in the sun. Tense-faced sentries stare down from a parapet, rifles trained over the heads of the crowd and a new machine gun post has been added, with a wide field of fire into the Chinese City. A path slices diagonally through all this, and Charlie and Fei are pushing along it, through the jagged shadows of the wire, nearly out the other side already.

In the crush, Ruby fights to keep them in view. It's going to be fine, she thinks. Nantao used to be as much home as the Settlement, it's just the old walled town at its heart that's dodgy. As long as they don't head through the remains of the old North Gate. She can hear Mother's voice now, adding her two pennyworth about where she was allowed to go – and where was forbidden – since Tom's death.

'That old part's *completely* out of bounds. At all times,' she snapped the last time Ruby was caught near there, and counted off the dangers on her nail-bitten fingers. 'Filthy. There's still a leper colony there, Ruby! Cholera. Rabid dogs. Besides, some days you can't find your own elbow, let alone negotiate a warren like that.'

'But I know how to keep safe,' Ruby pleaded. 'Don't eat anything that hasn't been cooked. Don't drink anything but hot tea—'

'The wind can change in a moment,' Dad rumbled. 'I don't have to remind you what an angry mob can be like, Ruby.'

No, she thought, you don't. But if Mum and Dad spoke some proper Chinese instead of just Pidgin, they'd understand the Chinese world better. It's not *unknowable, unpredictable*. Just different.

She's through the barrier now. Charlie and Fei are knifing through the tangle of rickshaws alongside the last remnants of the old wall – and she closes the gap to twenty or so paces, confident the crowd is thick enough to hide her even if they do glance round.

Sure enough they're heading for the gate. I'll follow a bit more, she thinks, and, at the first hint of trouble, I'll turn back.

The labyrinth of coiled streets in the old city is too tight even for the rickshaw men, and there's a scrum in front as pullers jockey to set down and pick up fares. Charlie glances round then, eyes sharp and quick as they sweep the crowd, and she ducks down. Too late? No, he hasn't seen her, and turns away leading Fei into deep shadow under the medieval gate.

Perhaps it's best to disguise myself, Ruby thinks. You don't get many Westerners in there at the moment. As she hurries after them she pulls the silk skull cap from her pocket, the one Amah gave her last birthday. 'Thirteen protectors,' Amah said, 'one for each year of your life.' The silver Buddhas embroidered on it wink in the sunlight as she crams it over her bob.

She's so intent on keeping her eyes on Charlie, that she doesn't spot the dark-suited men ahead of her. They've pulled to one side in a doorway, seemingly intent on lighting cigarettes in their cupped hands. But, as soon as Ruby has trotted past, they toss those to the floor and move back out into the street.

Following.

A different world envelops her, time shifting back a hundred years or more: no cars, no trams, no grand Western-style buildings, just knotted streets winding between two- and three-storey houses, snaking towards Nantao's hidden heart.

The air is hotter, clogged with spices and the stink of gutters. Wheelbarrow porters dodge past carrying mounds of coal, books, old ladies resting bound feet. Ruby feels drops of water on her cheek and looks up to see the sky shrunk to a narrow strip of blue, washing dripping from bamboo poles that reach across the narrow street. Cymbals and gongs sound on the air and a red sedan chair joggles past carrying its young bride inside like a hidden jewel. She steps back to let it go and then hurries on.

The Tangs are speeding up, alternately jogging a few steps, walking fast, then jogging again. Curiosity fully stoked, Ruby forgets to glance over her own shoulder as the streets close around her, and within minutes she starts to get the feeling she's swimming too far out of her depth. Like that time at the sea when the current got her, dragging her beyond the rolling, black waves and Dad had to thrash through the water to save her. She looks round to fix the route in her mind. Mustn't forget that shop, she thinks, looking at a cluster of birdcages hung on the front of a darkened building, sharp flashes of yellow and green fluttering inside bamboo cages.

You turn left here, she thinks. *Mei wenti. Mei wenti.*

When she looks back Charlie and Fei are almost out of sight. She races after them, past a pharmacy, baskets overflowing with dried snakes and blackened mushrooms. A man lurches from a doorway, grabbing her arms, spittle foaming the corner of his mouth as he rasps out a question. Ruby reels back, trying to keep spit out of her face, hearing Mother's warning loud in her ears.

'Sorry. I can't understand. Say it again?' she gasps, as much panicked about losing the others as by the strength of his grip.

The man's eyes are glazed from the dull emptiness of smoking opium. 'Touch my head, foreigner. Give me good luck – from your god.'

'Your gods are fine,' Ruby says hurriedly, reaching up to touch his bald head. 'But good luck, Uncle.'

The man nods, relaxing his grip and she wriggles free, turning to run after her friends, panic rising in her chest.

Blast it. I can't lose Charlie and Fei now . . .

But in the time it's taken to shake the man off, that is what *has* happened. She breaks into a run, glancing down each side alley, each open doorway, frantic for a glimpse of them.

Where on earth are they? She pauses to catch her breath at a small crossroads and peers down each street in turn. And which way is the gate? The sweat's in her eyes, stinging.

Is that them? Just a brief glimpse down a tiny alleyway, and she can't be sure, but enough of a lifeline that she grabs for it, running full pelt and cursing herself for being reckless enough to have ventured so far—

Then she trips. One moment she's up and running and the next she's caught a loose cobble and is flying, sprawling on the ground, skinning her knees, her hands bracing in a slick of some unidentifiable filth, as the shock jars her bones.

Blast it, blast it, blast it! She gets up quickly, checking herself over. The hem of her white dress is torn where it covers her knee and the skin underneath bloodied and dirty. The fear is back, taking hold, and she shivers despite the stifling heat, trying to control her breathing.

I've lost them.

Worse, she realizes, looking around, I haven't a clue where I am.

A few feet away a small dog with pale fur is standing motionless, panting gently. His face is alert and appealing, big eyes shining from under thick, wiry eyebrows, gazing at her. A thin line of drool spills from his chops. Hope it's not rabid, Ruby thinks, getting ready to fend off if it attacks.

But the dog just stands its ground, wagging his tail once or twice and staring at her.

'Go on, shoo, you old mutt,' she says, waving it away.

The animal turns obediently and trots away. But then it glances back over its shoulder and barks once loudly, waits a long moment, barks again and then slinks into the shadows. Beyond, at the far end of the alleyway from where she came, two figures are silhouetted.

They're moving towards her, Trilby hats bobbing as they quicken their pace.

'Missee?' the taller one of them calls. Then, in English: 'You need help? Missee?'

There's something more than concern in the man's voice, she thinks, some kind of edge that doesn't feel quite right. The kind of thing that demands you pay attention.

'We help you, Missee.'

Oh God, what now?

She turns, walking briskly away.

'Missee! Wait!'

The two men start to run, feet clomping the cobbles.

Survival instinct kicking, Ruby sprints away down the street as fast as she can, her pursuers' footsteps echoing loudly off the walls.

The day Dad rescued her from the water she had a brief glimpse of the enormity of the ocean. The waves enclosing her like walls, eager to drag her down as she swallowed the first cold mouthful. And below, something worse: a fathomless deep.

It feels like that now as she runs, hopelessly lost . . . down another side street, across a gloomy square, the footfall of her two pursuers beating fast and closing.

第八章

SWALLOW TAKES FLIGHT

Who on earth could they be?

At worst it could be slavers looking to kidnap her and take her upriver. Either for bargaining, or trading on into the chaotic Interior for ransom. Ruby's heard girls at school whispering stories to their stuck-up friends, and all of them shaking their heads darkly. But then that lot don't even know how babies are made. Probably just thieves looking to shake down an easy target for copper cash. Either way she doesn't want to hang around and find out.

She darts through an archway – and then sees that *same* scruff of a dog ahead of her, the light catching its straw-coloured fur. He looks at her from under those wiry eyebrows, barking loudly now as if trying to get her attention – and then seems to step *into* the wall and is gone.

How did it get there first?

As she draws level to where it disappeared, she sees a tiny slit between two buildings, so narrow the daylight hardly penetrates at all. The dog is as good as invisible, but she can hear the click of its claws as it retreats, and she squeezes into the narrow gap, between the mossy walls, trying to quieten the jabbering monkeys in her head and make herself small.

The footsteps are approaching fast, hesitating, then coming again at a sprint, and her heart beats harder against her ribs . . .

. . . but to her relief the two figures just lumber past, panting hard, blocking the light for a moment and then gone, the sound of their feet quickly fading.

She leans back against the wall, holding her breath, straining to make sure the men aren't doubling back. Despite cramming her hair under the skull cap, that's twice she's been picked as a foreign devil in the last few minutes. There's no hiding her colouring, the blue veined skin and freckles, the cornflower of her eyes. They just see that, she thinks. Not what's inside.

She waits another minute or so, regathering her scattered courage, reaching out again for Shanghai Ruby.

I'm OK. It was just careless to go down such an empty street in Nantao in the first place. My mistake.

Lucky that dog showing me the passageway, she thinks.

Away to her right she can hear raised voices, but a lot of them now, muddled together, and she turns towards the safety of the crowd. Round the next corner she runs slap into a dense throng. They're all facing one way, some lifting onto tiptoe to try and see what's going on, wheelbarrow porters and their passengers caught up in the jam. Everyone's craning their necks to see into a larger square ahead, wide enough for the sun to spill down on the people gathered there, voices edgy and loud. Someone pushes someone else and a small argument erupts.

The atmosphere feels jagged, nervous – the kind she's seen convulse streets before. Like that terrible, unforgettable day in Hankow. Something's about to happen and I've got to get out of here, she thinks, the wind's turning.

The glimpse of sunlight has gifted her some sense of direction. If the sun's up there, then crossing the square is roughly the right way towards the North Gate. Need to get past whatever's going on.

But progress is almost impossible. The bodies are packing tighter, and she struggles forward with difficulty, shoving her way through any gap or weak point in the crowd. Her eyes follow the gaze of the people around her, trying to work out what's going on

67

– and sees a young man standing on an upturned barrel, lifted clear of the crowd. He's drenched in light, his eyes shining and in the middle of delivering a speech of some kind. This far back his words are lost in the hubbub, but as Ruby edges further she starts to catch fragments of what he's saying:

'. . . only Communists can bring a better world, lift China up out of this filth . . .'

'. . . a ten thousand mile journey, comrades, starts with just one step . . .'

She pauses in her fight across the square, attention snagged by his energy.

'. . . the capitalists amongst our own people feed off the poor, sharing the meal with foreigners, while *our* workers rot in *their* factories. And don't *even* trust the Nationalists, my friends. They are no better than organized gangsters like the Green Hand.'

Most of the crowd bursts into applause, but a handful start shouting back, spitting obscenities at the young man and a wave of pushing and shoving convulses the audience, almost knocking Ruby off her feet. She has to brace to stop from going under.

Another voice rips the air. 'Don't listen to this *filth*!'

Ruby turns to see an older man scrambling onto a market stall. In his hand he's waving a rolled up newspaper, shaking it like a truncheon. 'Don't trust them,' he shouts. 'The Communists are liars. Here is a report of what they did to women and babies – *babies*! – in Shandong!'

Uproar seizes the crowd, some applauding, others booing, turning to see how the student on the barrel will respond. Ruby's caught in the middle of it all, dark waves rolling.

Above the young man's head there's a flash of blue as a lone swallow whisks out of the sky, diving down right past his face. He watches it climb again, then raises his hand to brandish a wodge of leaflets in the air.

'We can all be free. Let's not be like the man from Qi who feared the sky falling on his head!'

A good half of the crowd cheers loudly and then, fleetingly, behind the young radical, Ruby catches sight of Charlie and Fei.

All other thoughts go from her head. Saved! I'm saved, she thinks, if I can just get to them. She pushes forward again, hope soaring.

'Charlie!'

The Tangs are standing behind the student, watching him intently, and don't hear her over the uproar. Ruby raises her arm as high as she can, waving to get their attention – but her view is blocked as a fresh convulsion seizes the crowd. Screams erupt, and suddenly people are trying to run all ways at once.

In their haste, some stumble and fall – others, looking back over their shoulders, slam straight into Ruby, threatening to knock her to the ground. She fights to keep upright, pulled against her will towards where she came from, away from the Tangs.

Turning to look over her shoulder, she sees the space around the student has cleared, leaving him alone on his makeshift stage, looking around uncertainly. A new sound fills the air: the drumming of footsteps – and as people rush to get out of the way a squad of the local warlord's troops burst into the square.

Ruby recognises them from the cinema newsreel, a ragged bunch of ex-criminals, with weathered faces, hard eyes, their antique rifles gripped in bony hands. They look half-starved and the sun seems to slip past them without brightening their faces as they charge up to the young man and pull him from his barrel, snatching the leaflets. As he falls some of them flutter loose.

Something awful's coming.

She swallows hard. All thoughts of her predicament, of Charlie and Fei, are briefly eclipsed by the student's look of terror and helplessness. Oh God, Ruby thinks, please don't let them do something beastly to him.

It's too late. The soldiers are already pummelling the student with their gun butts, and, as the blows thud, the square falls silent. A few brave men move forward to try and help, but one of the soldiers fires over their heads, the whole crowd flinching as one, shrinking back.

Ruby groans. I wish I could help. But it's no use of course. If she had real *ch'i* powers she could push the soldiers away, fight them off like her heroine Hu San Niang saving the poor, the powerless . . .

At the same speed the troops entered the square, a giant of a man strides into view. He's dressed in black, his head covered by a hood, with just a slit for his eyes to show. Strapped across his back is an enormous, unsheathed broadsword, bright in the sun. Behind him, a short man with the face of a weasel is struggling to keep up. The magistrate.

Ruby's lips have gone dry. She knows what's coming.

Charlie has described a scene just like it a few months ago in a hushed voice, the dread still stamped on his face. I should go, she thinks, but her feet won't move. It's like she's mesmerised, can't pull them free of the ground, or her eyes away. The magistrate has unfurled a scroll and is reading from it in a fast, exaggerated voice ordering 'swift justice to fall like Heaven's fury on those who seek disorder'.

Ruby watches as the giant takes his broadsword and

holds it high, feels her own knees weakening as the student is forced to kneel. His face has lost all colour, but then he lifts his head and shouts: 'Rise up! Build a new China before—'

A soldier strikes him across the head, cutting his words short, stunning him into silence as the magistrate pronounces the single-word sentence.

'Death!'

The crowd murmur – and then there's a flicker of blue overhead. The swallow swooping low again, arcing past the student. He glances up to see it skim back into sunlight, into the vast ocean of sky above.

Then, with a horrible rush, it happens. The executioner brings the sword down, a flash of steel severing the man's head with a single blow. The crowd groans and Ruby shuts her eyes hard just a fraction too late, the image searing into memory – and when she opens her eyes again, the student's head has disappeared, like some gruesome magic trick, leaving his torso holding position for a second before it topples slowly forward.

For a moment Ruby's vision goes white, ears whooshing. She crouches to the ground, taking big gulps of air to fight off the faint that's threatening, and sees one of the student's leaflets at her feet. Without thinking, she reaches out for it.

China Awake! it says in big characters at the top. Then underneath: *One Day can be a Thousand Autumns*!

The magistrate is barking orders again, snapping her back to attention. As he raises a hand she sees a vivid flash of green glowing there.

'Arrest every communist sympathiser in the crowd!' he bellows. 'No mercy!'

She pulls the cap down harder on her head. On the one hand she knows as a foreigner she's immune from Chinese law, even in Nantao. On the other, she's heard enough stories of westerners slung into Chinese jails and left to rot for days before anyone found them. Sometimes the feared local magistrates act first and ask questions later.

It'll be OK. What does Dad call it? Extraterritoriality? What's the Chinese for that? Better just to run. Hope to find Charlie – but already chaos has gripped the crowd and it's twisting and turning around her like a whirlpool. She struggles to keep her feet as people are trampled, stumbling, steadying herself. A hand snatches the skullcap from her head.

'Hey, red devil!' someone yells. 'Clear off home!'

A space opens and she runs for it, trusting instinct to carry her to safety. Shots ring out, echoing off the tight walls. Stalls and alleys flash by, the crowds thinning for a moment, then choking again. In the next street, people seem to be hurrying the other way, their eyes wild. Are they fleeing some new horror – or from where she has just come? The sun's over there so that *must* be the right way. There's more gunfire behind her, and away to the left wild broken screaming.

At a quieter corner she pauses, doubled over, fighting for breath. If there's trouble in the Chinese City then the barricades will be closed and she'll be stuck on the wrong side. Got to keep moving.

She hears a bark then, a single sharp bark, and looks up astonished to see the straw-coloured dog again. His fur ruffles in a breeze, pulling her eyes with him as he turns down a side street, trotting through the scrum. Bewildered, but grateful to see what amounts to a friendly face, Ruby follows. A couple of turns later sees the shop with its wall of birdcages and bright finches and she runs again, overtaking the dog, running and running until somehow – gloriously – she sees the North Gate materialise in front of her and hurtles through it.

The streets are chaotic even outside the old walls, people racing for cover, pushing towards the checkpoint into the Settlement. But the barbed wire barricade has already been dragged across the road, and soldiers are mounting their parapet, levelling weapons at the advancing crowd.

Again she's caught up in the crush, and thinks for a moment that she's lost, being pulled under, but then a strong hand grabs her by the arm, tugging her free and she looks round to see a French soldier dragging her back towards the barrier. There's a chorus of catcalls and whistles from the rest of the crowd, cut short as the guards on the barrier fire above their heads.

'*Ça va, mademoiselle?*' the soldier asks, grimacing.

'Yes, yes, thank you,' Ruby gulps. '*Ça va.*'

'Go home,' he says, shaking his head, and sends her on her way with a shove. 'It's not safe.'

It seems completely unreal, but ten minutes later Ruby is standing breathless in their whitewashed hall, her figure blurry in the foxed depths of Mother's old mirror.

Dad is wrestling a bag of golf clubs, keen to get the most out of his *one damn day off*, the world as normal as normal could be.

'Where have you been, Ruby? Tangs?' he asks without looking up.

'Yes, I mean . . .' She trails off, her voice shaking.

Dad looks at her sharply. 'What have you done? Get clean before Mother sees!'

Somewhere out over the East China Sea the thunder rumbles long and loud, trembling the new windows in their metal frames: the daily storm starting its advance.

'I'm sorry, I—'

'Never mind. Just get clean.'

Ruby stands for a moment in the hall, her mind reeling, and then goes slowly to the bathroom. She has seen plenty of dead bodies on the street before, dogs tugging at beggars who died on their doorstep in Bubbling Well Road. As a small child she used to bury the bodies of dead animals – even an abandoned new-born baby once on the Wilderness.

And Tom's body laid out in the funeral parlour, of course – about to embark on his journey in the coffin to who knows where.

But nothing has prepared her for that terrifying moment in the square. She feels a grainy sting behind her eyelids and screws her mouth up, fists tightening.

'You must not cry,' Mother said, gripping her tightly in the days after his death. 'You mustn't. Tom wouldn't want you to, I don't want you to . . .'

And so she hasn't ever really done so, even though she and Tom were inseparable, hardly ever apart. Like *yin* and *yang* Amah used to say: where one of you is, there's always a bit of the other, even when you're fighting.

Ruby's breath catches, that plum stone jammed in her throat again.

Tom.

She tries to pull her mind away from the thought, balling her fists even tighter so she can feel the nails digging into her palms – but the death of the student has brought Tom firmly back again. Where is he now? Drifting in the Otherworld, with all those other lost and troubled souls, the restless spirits? It doesn't bear thinking about.

She reaches for the talisman in her pocket – and is surprised to find the student's leaflet tucked there with it, scuffed and muddied, the bold black characters still shouting their defiant message. Don't remember putting it there, she thinks, holding it with trembling fingers.

China Awake! One day can be a thousand autumns if we act now!

And then there's violent hammering on the front door.

第九章

CROSS MY HEART

She folds the leaflet and jams it back in the pocket of her dress along with the precious talisman, as the drumming on the door comes again. She can hear Father stumping to answer, his leg heavy as he growls: 'I'm coming, blast it!'

Maybe it's the police from the checkpoint and they'll give her away? Or Charlie come to see I'm OK? He's hardly ever visited the flat, but he knows where it is. Maybe he saw me in the crowd, she thinks, hopes rising, but as she nudges the door open and listens to the voices in the hall, that possibility is snuffed out.

Dad's words are forceful, angry even, as he fires Pidgin English at whoever's at the door. 'You not belong this side place! I told you already. Savvy?'

She can't make out the response, but the nasal voice

certainly doesn't belong to Charlie, or anyone else she knows. A staccato Chinese, tones exaggerated.

Dad again, his voice calmer but still firm: 'You go now. Belong Nantao side.'

Without a sound, Ruby edges out into the corridor. Dad has his back to her, and the front door is open on the chain, blocking any glimpse of whoever is standing the other side.

She catches a fragment of the Chinese voice. 'I go where I want. Answer question.'

'You have one minute to get out of the building,' Dad says. 'Or I call the police. I have *no* blessed idea where she is. Savvy?'

He's standing in an odd way, trying to keep his weight off his bad leg, but his right hand, the one not holding the doorknob, stretches out to the coat stand, and is thrust deep in his overcoat pocket all the time he's talking to the man.

Thin voice comes again. 'No problem. I go now.'

'That's the spirit. Tell your boss I'll come. When I'm ready.'

There's the sound of receding footsteps. Dad waits, the door still gapped, and then closes it softly. He hesitates, takes his hand from his coat pocket and draws a long, deep breath, before swinging round. He looks startled to see Ruby, but then gathers himself.

'Didn't we teach you not to eavesdrop, Ruby?'

'I – who was that?'

'Just some blessed beggar. I'll have to speak to the guard.'

'Who was he looking for?'

'Some – woman. On another floor,' Dad stumbles, then looks at her. 'You are alright aren't you, Ruby?' he adds, his voice just a bit softer. And tired.

Ruby puts on a brave face. 'I'm fine. Cross my heart and hope to die.'

'Hope not!' Dad smiles. 'That's what my Shanghai Ruby always used to say, and then I'd find out you'd been in some awful scrape or other. Always sticking up for lost causes . . .' He glances out the window, adding softly: 'You know what, perhaps I'll not bother with golf after all. Looks like rain. Let's keep company.'

An hour later the sky has darkened, the clouds' heavy undersides bulging as they drift across the river, the grand buildings, the shanties and suburbs. Ruby is at her spot by the window, fretting about Charlie and Fei. A lightning bolt connects sky and earth out past the factories in Pudong, sun bright.

Ghosts and foxes have slipped from her mind as she recalls the look on Charlie's face as he and Fei set out from the temple this morning. There aren't meant

80

to be any secrets in the Society: the Tangs will just have to cough up and tell. It can't wait until tomorrow, and school's just days away with its catcalls and awkwardness.

The rain starts to fall. Dad's looking frustrated himself, slumped in an armchair.

'Can I just go out for a minute?' Ruby asks, as innocently as she can.

'In this weather? And do what?'

'Just want to go to Uchiyama's. I'm bored.'

Father screws up his face in thought, then nods.

'OK. Straight there and straight back. Nowhere else. Five at the very latest.'

'Where's Mother?'

'God only knows,' Dad says. He goes to add something but then cuts himself short. 'Don't be late—'

'Thanks!' Ruby beams. 'I'll take a coat.'

He waves a hand in the air and then sinks back in the chair with a sigh.

She hesitates. 'Dad?'

'Hello.'

'Are *you* OK?'

'Yes. I'm fine. Just have a care, will you?'

'I will.'

She grabs her mac from the stand by the door,

wonders briefly again about how Dad stood with his hand thrust in his coat pocket, and then hurries to the lift.

The streets around the Tangs' alleyway house are familiar ground, but today they feel changed. Shadows in doorways seem darker, the rain harder on her face when she glances up, and the looks from passers-by more direct, even a bit hostile. Feels a bit like those last few days when they were living at the treaty port in Hankow, she thinks. Tom and I walking to the river to fish and watch the tame cormorants shaking out and drying their wings. Tom mimicked them and fell in, and we laughed all the way home, but you could feel the looks on people's faces changing around us. Getting harder. You could feel it coming.

But I'm safe here, surely. *Mei wenti.*

At the corner to Bright Pond Road she pauses, peering through the rain towards the Tangs. No lights in the downstairs window and the door stands shut against the weather. Normally she'd rush up and knock loudly on it, eager for the front room overflowing with life and hot tea, but today she hesitates an extra heartbeat or two before slipping down the cobbled street.

The rain comes harder, obscuring her vision and

she ducks into a doorway on the other side of the alleyway for shelter. Something moves then, away to her right, further down. Is that a shadow, or a figure pressed tight against the wall, behind a curtain of water spilling from the foaming gutter above? She squints through the rain. No – nothing there. She pulls the hood over her head, before splashing through the puddles to the Tangs' door, rapping on it hard.

As she waits, she glances around, and sees a face materialise in a darkened window behind – just a blur and then it's snuffed out again. That's where the old lady – who always shares sticky red bean gum with them – lives. But she's normally friendly, beckoning me in for a gossip . . .

Ruby bangs on the Tang's door, harder this time, then calls out. '*Ni hao?* It's me! *Ni zai na li?*'

Where *are* you all? she thinks, rattling the handle. The door won't budge, so she dodges into the rain again and presses her face to the downstairs window. It's completely dark inside and impossible to see anything through the water and gloom, but then the lightning stutters and the sitting room is illuminated to reveal Mister Tang crouched by the big table looking her way, his mouth opening in surprise – or alarm. She taps on the wet glass and calls over the sound of the rain. 'Can I come in?'

Mister Tang hesitates, then straightens up and makes his way quickly towards the door.

By the time Ruby is dripping in the hallway, he seems to have recovered something of his usual good humour and calm. Or at least he's making an effort to do so. He ushers her in, rubbing the back of his head like he does when trying to solve a problem with his writing.

'Ah, it's you, Ruby. Come in, come in. Come out of that terrible weather. Gods must be punishing us for something. I'd offer you some tea, or a snack, but I'm in a bit of a hurry, I'm sorry to say.'

He closes the door firmly and then turns the key in the lock before pushing his back to the wood, sighing out a long breath.

'Sorry to bother you,' Ruby says, eyes roving the room. The atmosphere inside doesn't feel right at all, the room devoid of its usual life and buzz. 'Are Charlie and Fei in? We were meant to meet this afternoon but they didn't show up.'

A suitcase stands open on the table. It's half filled with clothes, a few books, a sheaf of paper covered in Mister Tang's tiny handwriting.

He follows Ruby's gaze. 'As you can see I'm just going off to Shandong. For a few days,' he says quickly. 'Going to interview a writer there. Charlie and Fei are coming with me to see some relatives. They're at the North Station already, I hope.' He smiles, trying to make that smile as big and reassuring as ever.

'They never mentioned it!'

She doesn't mean the words to come out so abruptly. 'I mean they normally tell me—'

Mister Tang holds up his hands, like someone surrendering. 'Last minute plan. I really would offer you something, but I've got to dash or I'll miss the train, Ruby. We'll miss the train,'

'That's OK,' she says, voice faltering. She doesn't quite believe him. Charlie always laughs that his dad is terrible at telling lies. But either way it means her friends have been keeping even more from her: either they *are* off to Shandong and didn't say, or who knows where they are. She needs to know what's going on, and fumbles to stall for another minute or so. Mister Tang will blurt out the truth if Charlie's right. He always does, apparently.

'Did Charlie and Fei tell you about us catching a ghost.'

Mister Tang looks totally wrong-footed, his forehead ridging as he tries to understand. 'Ghost? A game you mean?'

'No! A real one! We trapped a fox at the temple and chucked it down the well—'

'Well good for you,' Tang says absently. 'Poor old ghost . . .'

'It was real!' Ruby insists. 'Charlie and Fei saw it too!'

Mister Tang hesitates, rubbing the back of his head again and turns to face Ruby. 'You're a good girl, Ruby. We all love you. And you're smart too. But a word of advice? Be careful about letting your imagination run loose. Once it gets going there's no stopping it. You had a bad shock last year and nobody – almost nobody – can go through things like that without some effect on their thinking—'

'But—'

'Be careful you don't get washed away by the rubbish that's kept this country in the dark for far too long.'

'But we saw it!'

Mister Tang opens his mouth to argue, but then glances at his watch.

'I really must go. Any message for my two rascals?'

Ruby shakes her head.

'Just say hello. Have a good trip,' she says, remembering her manners, feeling suddenly light in the head and rather dizzy. She reaches out a hand to steady herself.

Mister Tang hesitates, as if regretting his lecture.

'Well, who knows what you saw, eh? The year after my dear wife died, in the famine of '20, I was sitting here in this very room, and – well – I saw her walk past that window.' He nods at the rain-lashed panes. 'But of course it's just because I wanted to see her. So badly.'

'Maybe she was really there,' Ruby says.

'I don't think so,' Mister Tang says sadly. 'Now, if anyone's asking about me, be sure to let them know I've gone to Shandong won't you? Shandong, got that?'

With that he unlocks the door and pretty much shoves her back out into the tumbling rain.

As the door closes behind her, a cold ripple bumps each and every vertebrae in her spine. Not like when the ghosts are near, more like she's going down with something, a cold or flu. I've pushed my luck enough. Can't face Mother and all that fuss if I get ill.

She eyes the house again, wondering if she should wait and follow Mister Tang, but after five minutes there's no sign, and feeling more and more shivery by the minute, she decides to give up and head for home. At least after a quick swing by White Cloud just in case any of the others are there. No harm in that . . .

Ruby trots on in the rain, legs feeling wobbly and

weak. So hard to tell sometimes if it's the ground moving, or you, the air vibrating from a distant explosion, or your own nerves jangling. She glances up and it's like the clouds sway down at her, suddenly massive and suffocating, and she falls . . .

第十章

DARK JUNK, DISTANT RIVER

A dream – or something like a dream – plays in her confused head.

She sees that familiar, silvery river snaking into the gloom across a vast plain. But now the vision is more detailed.

She's gliding over the water, high up. You can see mountains in the distance, but the sky is getting thicker and blacker. Slowly she loses speed, drifting down lower towards the water, lower, struggling to regain height. There's a boat on the river ahead – a small dark junk plugging towards her through the mist. It looks abandoned, not a soul on the deck. As she slides down through the cold air she realizes she's heading for it, her approach angled like a plane aiming for a tiny landing strip. She hears the sails creak through the mist and then her feet touch the boards, landing softly amongst the clutter of coiled rope and barrels. The wind moans through the rigging and she makes her way to the stern. A heavy Chinese style coffin is lying on blocks there, raised as if in offering to the sky. Fear creeps through her, into her veins, into the roots of her hair, into her stomach as she approaches slowly. And then she hears another sound, something halfway between a cough and a bark, and when she spins around she finds herself looking straight into the face of a fox.

It looks old and fierce, fur streaked with silver, bristling with energy, long teeth visible as it opens its mouth—

Skksssshhhhhh.

There's a noise like paper being ripped next to her ear, and the fox and the coffin and the river are gone in a flash of light. She opens her eyes to dazzling brightness and to see Mother standing there tapping her front teeth with her fingernail. When she sees Ruby's eyelids flicker open, she lets out a gasp.

'Thank God.'

Ruby scrunches her eyes against the light, sees the curtains swaying from being drawn, the look of anguish on her mother's face. She feels her body heat now and struggles to kick the cover off. Somehow the fox's face – so strong, so brimming with urgency – is still staring at her, floating before her in the room.

'What happened?'

'You fainted, my girl. That's what happened. And you've got a fever. Doctor Sprick was here last night and he's coming back this morning. I just hope to God it's not something—'

Mother jams her brakes on, but the usual worry and fear has already filled the room.

'You'll be OK. But it's bed for you for a few days. Absolute rest and NO going out. Hear me?'

'But I need to find Charlie and Fei,' Ruby mutters, her voice shaky.

'No chance. Your father's at work, but I'm staying right here with you.'

'What time is it?'

'Ten thirty.'

'But it's light.'

'Ten thirty in the morning silly. You've been spark out since last evening when they found you in a puddle.'

'Who found me?'

'Some dirty rickshaw man. And then they took you to Central Police Station and luckily – luckily – one of the sergeants recognised you from the Council Christmas party last year . . . God only knows what might have happened otherwise.'

Ruby groans, pulling the covers over her. 'I'm fine. Tell Doctor Sprick not to bother—'

'You are in no position to argue, young lady. Now get some rest and let the fever run its course—'

Out of her fogged head an urgent thought crystallises. 'Where's my dress?'

'What do you mean?'

'The one I was wearing yesterday. I need something from the pocket.'

'In the wash. There was nothing in the pocket but a scrap with scribbling all over it. It was soaked so I tossed it . . .'

Ruby groans again. The talisman, gone.

'But I *needed* it!'

'The only thing you need is a dose of common sense. You're an accident waiting to happen.'

'Can you draw the curtains again?'

Mother's voice softens. 'You need some light. You're as pale as anything.'

There's a knock on the front door and she spins away to answer it, finger back at her teeth, tapping them. 'That'll be the doctor.'

But it's not Doctor Sprick who enters a minute or so later.

'Miss Harkner?'

A broad-shouldered man fills the doorway to her room. His features are curiously indistinct, as if someone's drawn them, rubbed them out, then sketched them back again. The effect is unsettling, as is the smile on his face that seems added as an afterthought. He's holding his hat with both hands in front of him, working it in his fingers as he peers at Ruby.

'Do excuse me, young lady,' he says, his voice deep, an American accent dragging the syllables. 'You all OK now?'

Mother hovers behind him, her voice pitched up a note, strained. 'But surely it can wait—'

'It really won't take a moment.' The man raises his eyebrows at Ruby, then throws her a wink, trying to catch her interest.

'Who did you say you were again?' Mother says.

'George Woods. American Intelligence. You've *seen* my card, Mrs Harkner. Would you like to phone my superiors on the number shown there?'

'But what could you want with Ruby?'

'She had something interesting on her, when she was handed into the police last night. I'm just curious to find out where she got it. And who gave it to her. Et cetera.'

Ruby tenses then under the covers. Does he mean

the talisman? What would he care about that?

But then she remembers the student's crumpled leaflet, and she sits up, trying to clear her head, to focus on what to say. Not the truth. Not quite, she's sure of that. She's awake enough to know that something about the Nantao trip – about Charlie and Fei and their dad – feels wrong.

'Interesting?' Mother says like a flustered parrot.

Woods ignores her. 'I really don't want to bother you for long Miss Harkner, but I just need to ask you a couple of questions. May I?' he gestures with his hat at the foot of the bed and then sits down without waiting for an answer, like someone who's used to getting his way. Ruby recognises him now – she's seen him in the lift a couple of times, raising his hat at her in a way that could be sincere, but could be mocking. Dad said he was a geologist or something.

'I thought . . . you were working for a petroleum company.'

'You've blown my cover, Miss Harkner,' he smiles. 'No. I'm a special kind of policeman. I'm keeping an eye on who's doing what here in Shanghai – and I was at Foochow Road police station when they brought you in.'

'I thought you'd only just come to Shanghai.'

'I've been here a few weeks.'

'Then you can't possibly hope to know what's going on,' Ruby says, puffing out her cheeks. 'You have to have lived here all your life if you want to do that.'

'Well, perhaps you can help me then if you're such an expert,' he says, inclining his head, grinning. 'When the police were looking for your identity last night they found a leaflet in your pocket. A piece of Communist propaganda. I just need to know where you got it. I expect you just kept it because it looked exciting, we obviously don't think you have any business with people like that!'

'People like what?'

'Dangerous people, who want to bring all this' – Woods sweeps his hand in a circle indicating the city, the world – 'crashing down in flames.'

Ruby looks at him, full into that battered face. There's something rather likeable there now, a playful gleam in the eyes. But still – better to be careful.

'I was near the barricade to the Chinese City yesterday,' she says slowly. 'And there was trouble so I didn't want to get too close. People were running back through the checkpoint and one of them dropped the leaflet. I picked it up to see what it was – and I must have put it in my pocket.'

Woods eyebrows knit together as if he's trying to

95

work out a tricky mathematics problem. He takes a sharp breath.

'OK. *Pretty* much what I guessed. You didn't see *who* dropped it?'

'Come on now,' Mother says, irritably. 'You can't expect her to pick one of *them* out in a fleeing crowd.'

Ruby scowls at her mother.

'She seems like a pretty sharp young lady,' Woods says, holding up his hand.

'I didn't see who dropped it.'

Woods gets up. 'Well, you get some rest, Miss Harkner. Keep clear of Nantao if I was you. It's all going to get a lot messier before it gets better.'

He walks to the door, nods at Mother – and pauses.

Then he astonishes Ruby by coming out with a sentence in perfect Chinese, carefully picking out the rising and falling tones: 'If I were you I would choose my friends very carefully right now.'

'*Xie xie*. Thank you,' Ruby says, flummoxed. She had him picked for one of those typical 'adventurer' types who never bother to learn the language. She rolls over, wondering what he knows. What he meant about 'friends'.

A few moments later, after heated words in the hallway, Mother returns. 'What did he say to you? In Chinese?'

'He just said "get better soon".' Ruby says, flustered. She can feel the heat building in her head and hands and feet, her pulse drumming.

'How many times have I told you not to pick up filthy things in the street?' Mother says as she sweeps back out of the room. 'How *many* times?'

'Hundreds,' Ruby whispers, closing her eyes and feigning the drift towards sleep. She needs a moment to herself to think, needs some peace and quiet to work out what to do next. 'I'm sorry.'

What's that Chinese proverb Mister Tang always quotes? *When one person lies, a hundred repeat it as true.*

第十一章

OFFERINGS TO HEAVEN

For an hour or so her mind works against the growing temperature cooking the bedclothes. Each time she tries to focus, her concentration slips. As she feels the heat build, she worries that maybe she really is ill with something awful like typhoid or dysentery. No, it can't be. It's just a flu, a summer cold, no more than that. But then this is just how it started with Tom after he fell in the river . . .

In the grip of fever she rolls over and stares at the ceiling, the clock ticking, sweat running. She blinks. The plaster overhead ripples and blurs as she does so – and somehow becomes the summer sky over Hankow: the brown, hot, clouds, the swallows sweeping arcs and flicking the surface of the mighty Yangtze. Her memories are running, and the fever muddles past and present, so that she's back in the last days of their stay upriver. Tom lying pasty and sweating on the bed, his eyes looking far, far away, Mother curled at his feet, Dad pacing. Outside the window there's the sound of distant gunshots, sharp little coughs that echo off the walls, and on the horizon a line of pale green willows and reeds where the river banks run. The gunboat is still a day away from coming to their rescue and the treaty port staff are outside murmuring disquiet.

Quite distinctly, she hears Tom's voice like she heard it that day: *I can see a boat on the river. I need to get on it, Ruby. I can't miss it.*

Terrified by the note in his words, she makes her mind up at long last, jumps out the window, and speeds off down the hot street to try and find the doctor, her feet kicking brown dust under the immense sky, trying to ignore the gunfire and chanting just streets away. If only her legs would work properly, but it feels like they're tangled up under her as the gunfire crackles again.

'It's a race against time,' Ruby hears her own voice mumbling as she lapses back into fitful sleep.

On the edge of dream, she hears the rattling, tinny clap of Tom's wind-up monkey coming from somewhere that sounds both close up – and far away. And someone calling her name over and over again, the two syllables insistent, rhythmic in her ear.

It could be hours or days or just minutes later when she wakes with a start, disorientated, looking around for that chattering monkey with its brass cymbals.

Outside the sky has clouded again, but this time into an unbroken sheet of dull lead. No thunder today, maybe even the first hint of autumn carried with it. Her pillow and sheets are damp with sweat, but the heat has lifted from her body, and she feels better. Much better. Her legs twitch like they've been running for hours, knotting the sheets with a lung-busting effort to get somewhere. To *do* something.

'Amah?' she calls. 'Mum?'

Silence answers her.

Then pricking that, from far off there's a sound like seedpods popping in the sun. It can't be firecrackers – the pattern's all wrong for that. More like gunfire, but miles and miles away. Outside the city.

Ruby slips barefoot across the room and creeps into the hall. Not a sound in the flat, except a familiar rhythmic breathing that tells her Amah has fallen asleep on guard duty. Sure enough she finds the old lady slumped in Dad's armchair in the sitting room, her small, wrapped feet propped on the stool, mouth open. Maybe I should wake her up? she thinks. I could see if she knows anything about what Charlie and Fei or their dad is up to? No. This might be the only chance to get away to the temple and find the others before school cramps her life again. Amah would sympathise, but she won't dare go against Mother.

She hurries back to the bedroom, and gets dressed, then grabs three silver dollars from the pot on the mantelpiece and scribbles a quick note.

GONE FOR A WALK. BACK IN TEN MINUTES.

She looks at it for a moment and then adds:

FEELING BETTER. R x

It won't save her from punishment, but it might soften it a bit.

She tiptoes down the hall and slips on her shoes. As she passes the antique mirror, she glances into its mottled surface, wondering whether she still looks ill. She's always liked the looking glass, the way the surface plays with your reflection.

Peering into the depths she sees her uncertain features staring back at her, anxiety and dark rings clear to see—

And then everything feels very odd, as if a space has opened behind her. There's an overwhelming vertigo, like she might fall backwards into an immense depth, and she sees something – or someone – standing right by her shoulder. So quick she can't register who or what it is, but *definitely* something behind her, a shadowy figure about her height, and she spins round, skin fizzing like it does when the ghosts are close by, sweeping her hand to ward the thing off.

Nothing. No one.

All the way to White Cloud the back of her head feels twitchy, as if someone has eyes glued to the back of it, or binoculars or even a gunsight lined up there. Twice she turns round abruptly, trying to surprise whoever or whatever it is. But if anything the streets seem emptier than normal.

Mother just shouldn't have chucked the talisman without asking. Now with it gone, it's no wonder something's come back to the apartment. I'm going to have to get Yu Lan to do the calligraphy again, she thinks. If he's not at the temple I'll have to go to his house on Rue du Consulat. But the bodyguards there turn most people away, she knows that. And Yu says they're a rough bunch: ex-convicts, and another is a disgraced British policeman who drowned a beggar in Soochow Creek once. But she *needs* that talisman. Otherwise who knows what will happen tonight.

Overhead a bi-plane detaches itself from the the

sky, black in the dull afternoon, and wobbles towards the horizon, trailing a banner that says '*The all new GREAT WORLD. Full of surprises!*'

When she reaches it, the temple seems gripped in even deeper hush than normal. The bamboo towering over the back wall sways in the faintest of breezes, its soft hiss the only sound. Despite the fever going, she still feels tired, and instead of scrambling over the usual way she makes her way to the old gate at the front. The doors under the carved porch have been boarded up for years, but there's a loose plank you can just squeeze past.

But as she approaches Ruby sees some of the boards have been yanked away, and a gaping hole gives a clear view into the courtyard. She looks up and down the road, concerned, waits until no one is watching and then slips through the gap.

Inside, everything looks normal.

Weeds and thistly seedheads, the well with its broken bucket, the watching dead on their stones.

'*Ni hao*?' she calls softly. 'Anyone here?'

There's incense on the air and – hope rising – she nips across the courtyard and hops up the two steps into the main hall, the boards shifting beneath her weight.

'Charlie?'

No one there, but eyes adjusting to the gloom, she sees something that gives her another jolt. The altar – which for so long has been empty and a place to sit and chat – is now laden with offerings: a heap of sunburst oranges, a vase stuffed with bubbling white chrysanthemums. Three expensive bundles of cedar incense are sending smoke to the dragons and fading painted clouds above. Two red candles light up the statue of the Jade Emperor behind. Normally she doesn't see his plasterwork – just part of the decor – but those flames seem to have put life into his stern features, his eyebrows gathered as if he's just asked Ruby a question.

Have the others done this? If so, they should have waited for her.

Something taps her on the shoulder, startling her, and she wheels round expecting – fearing – anything: drunken beggar, the fox spirit returning, a policeman.

But it's Andrei. He flicks a bright smile and raises his hands in apology. 'Not mean scare you, Ruby. Sorry.'

'What's going on?' she whispers, trying to calm her jumping heart. 'Where are the others?'

'Don't know. But some man sleeping there,' he jerks his thumb at the monks' corridor beyond.

'And now all this candle and stuff.'

'Have you seen Charlie—?'

A series of violent bangs ring out overhead, shaking fresh plaster loose. Andrei's eyes are as wide as hers. 'Mama says bad thing coming to Shanghai.' He looks up at the roof. 'Really terrible thing—'

'Shhh.'

There's another sound now, like something big and stealthy moving along the ridge tiles. Then three more loud thumps, and something crashes down in the courtyard.

'Come on,' Ruby says, grabbing Andrei, pulling him back out into the light.

Four or five ridge tiles lie smashed amongst the weeds, rust coloured fragments scattered amongst the green. Ruby turns to look back at the roof, and sees a figure standing there, dramatically silhouetted against the brighter sky.

Dumbfound, she watches as its arms separate slowly from the body, like one of those Yangtze cormorants drying its wings, and then it lifts its head to show a beaten-up black hat, a man's face shadowed beneath. For a moment the figure is *absolutely* still – and then snaps into motion.

Ruby and Andrei both gasp, backing away as he comes hurtling down the roof towards them – and vaults clean into the air. He drops to the porch over the main door, takes two more powerful strides that rattle the tiles, and punches into a loosely tucked somersault, dark clothes flapping as he turns. With a thud the dark figure lands right before them, his head bowed, one strong fist held in the other in Chinese greeting – and is motionless again.

Ruby holds her breath, and waits, until at last the man raises his head, to reveal a strong jaw, the hint of a smile, not a trace of effort snagging his breath. Under the brim of his battered Fedora, the eyes are bright, alive with energy and vitality. They reach out and lock onto hers. Then he sweeps the hat from his head spilling straggly, black hair veined with silver, like moonlight running on the edges of midnight clouds.

'Very good to meet you properly at last,' he says in a croaky voice, tapping the hat back into place, and advances towards her with rapid strides, not once breaking that eye contact. 'It's time we had a good chat, Miss Harkner.'

第十二章

LAO JIN

The man coughs, reaching up with a powerful hand to massage his Adam's apple. He's Chinese, maybe in his thirties or forties, but it's hard to tell. Not quite young, not quite old.

Around his eyes the lines are packed like someone who's worked outdoors all his life and his skin has the polished, coppery look the older rickshaw men have. But his movements and posture are young and light as he crosses the ground quickly towards her.

Ruby wonders if she should be backing away, turning and running even, but when she tries to pull her eyes from his gaze, she finds that she can't. No, it's not quite that, more that she doesn't want to. Something in those eyes is speaking to her. *Mei wenti*, *Ruby*, a voice mutters in her head.

'An honour to meet you,' the stranger smiles, as he

pushes out the Shanghai dialect. But there's another accent cutting against that, like someone from up beyond Nanking, a hint of Hubei province or even further up the Yangtze.

'Who are you?' Ruby says. 'What are you doing in our temple?'

He spits out a gob of muck. 'Your temple? It belongs to everyone Ruby. Everyone. Or no one.'

'How do you know my name?'

'Really nobody owns anything do they? We just look after things for a bit. That's what my master always said when I was training.' His voice is smoother now, coming more easily as he looks round the courtyard. 'You and your friends have been doing a good job with this old place. And now I'm here to help.'

Ruby bites her lip. 'I said: *how* do you know my name?'

'And who hell are you, old man?' Andrei adds, his voice on edge.

The stranger glances at him, smile widening. 'I'm the new guardian of the temple. Glorified caretaker! Why don't we go inside and have a chat?'

Ruby shakes her head. She's had enough of people who seem to know better than her. All those knowing looks from Mister Tang, Dad, Woods – and now this man, as if she's the last to know a vital secret about the world.

'Not until you tell me *how* you know my name,' she says, doggedly returning his gaze.

The man cocks his head, the sinews in his neck rippling.

'You must forgive me. I suppose I've been spying on you.' He nods at the main building. 'I've been kipping in the old cells for a few nights and I heard you lot telling ghost stories the other day. Good stuff! That one about the old hag who hid in the skin of a young woman. I remember my dad telling me that one years ago. *Years* ago!'

A shadow slips across his face – then his smile is back. 'My name's Jin. Lao Jin. I've come to clean the place up.'

'But why?' Andrei says. 'No one wants it these days – not until they knock down and make a hotel or something.'

'Some places aren't suitable for new buildings. Unstable. They had to stand the new French bank on forty-foot piles and it's still sinking. Maybe it'll go right under! Wouldn't that be good! And some very important people want to get this place spick and span again.'

Ruby's still holding his gaze, but her caution is

wavering. Something in those playful eyes is softening her, firing her curiosity again. 'Like who?'

'People you don't say "no" to,' the man says, and turns abruptly towards the main hall.

'But this has been our place for *ages*. We even chased a fox out of here the other day.'

Jin stops in his tracks, shaking his head slowly. 'A fox? Not sure such what I think about that. Just stories wouldn't you say? But maybe I can help you a bit.'

'We don't need help,' Ruby says. 'I mean, thank you – but, but we're OK, we've got something to help us.'

Best not to tell a stranger about the Almanac though. Her eyes flicker away to the hiding place, and back to find Jin's resting intently on hers again.

'Can't trust everyone or everything that promises to help to be *reliable*,' he says, picking the last word out carefully.

'Where did you learn all that stuff,' Andrei breaks in, weaving his hand in imitation of Jin's acrobatics.

'You like that? I used to be in training at Shaolin. And other places.'

'Shaolin?' Andrei gasps, interest spiked by the mention of the famous martial arts' temple.

'A lifetime ago, but I still remember a bit,' Jin says,

and is suddenly moving, hands, legs snaking as he circles them both, feinting then fist striking with a snap, before dropping into a low powerful kick. His movements are full of energy and yet relaxed, smooth but fast, feet sweeping the boards as if only just touching them. And then he leaps high in the air, higher than you'd think a man could jump, and seems to hover for an extra moment before he lands elegantly, breathing slightly faster now – and laughs at the look plastered on both Ruby and Andrei's faces.

'Close your mouths. You'll catch flies,' he laughs. 'I'm a bit rusty. Been cooped up a long time.'

Andrei shakes his head. 'You're a weird kind of caretaker.'

'Caretaker, watchman, guardian,' Jin says crisply. 'A couple of other things too. We all get to play a few parts in our lives, wouldn't you say? Take you: one day you're the son of a rich Russian businessman in Saint Petersburg, the next you're slogging across Siberia to become a beggar in Shanghai.'

Andrei frowns. 'How do you know that?'

'Most things are obvious if you look properly. For example,' his eyes shift back to Ruby, 'you've had a great fright recently. Not just your silly old fox, but something else. Am I right?'

Ruby shifts uncomfortably. 'What do you mean?'

Jin seems fascinating, as if he is a figure striding from the pages of *Outlaws of the Marsh*. But how does he know so much about them? There's a wild edge to him, to the way he speaks, a bit like when people have had too much to drink. Maybe it's better just to try and find Yu and get the talisman done – or spend what little time she has combing the streets for the Tangs.

'I really need to get home,' Ruby says.

'We need to have a talk. I can see you're troubled. Your friends too.'

She returns his gaze, that pulse in his eyes searching for something. Fishing.

He grins. 'Tell me more about your fox, for example?'

'We got rid of it.'

'Can you teach us to fight like that?' Andrei interrupts. 'Do jumps and kicks?'

'I could show you some basics. But you have to help me in return.'

'Like what?'

'Cleaning,' Jin sighs. 'Meet me back here tomorrow. I'd like to meet Charlie and Fei. I know someone who used to know their dad . . .'

Ruby's unease stirs again. There's danger around the Tangs, and although she hasn't a clue what it is, she can guess it's not good to go blabbing what little she does know to every stranger she meets.

'I'm not sure where they are,' she says quickly. 'I think they've gone away.'

'I doubt it! I think they'll be here tomorrow. Shall we say nine o'clock?'

'I don't think I'll—'

'You'll be here,' Jin says resolutely. 'Things are changing. You need to know that.'

Ruby looks around at the broken glory of White Cloud. Only now is it hitting home what the stranger has said about the temple reopening.

'Who's the new owner?'

Jin's face darkens again a little, his eyes narrowing.

'Ever heard of an old bastard called Moonface?' he asks.

Ruby's heart sinks, and beside her Andrei groans as if punched.

'Exactly,' Jin says. 'He and some foreigners have bought the place from the Association. Not sure why. But at least I've got a job at last. Beggars can't be choosers, not right now.'

'So you are working for *him*?' Andrei spits.

'He's paying me. But I wouldn't say I was working for him,' Jin says. He tilts his head sharply, listening. 'And his car's just drawing up at the front gate. You two better make yourselves scarce.'

There's the *poom, poom* of car doors slamming by the front gate.

'Go on. We'll see each other tomorrow.'

Something in Jin's fiery energy is still holding Ruby, but he's already turned away, walking across the courtyard. As he goes his posture slumps, as if he's aging right before her eyes. One shoulder sags and from a pocket he pulls a grubby bottle and takes a swig.

Andrei's tugging at her sleeve.

'Come on! Let's go!'

She takes one last look as figures darken the gap in the gates and rough voices call out.

'Oi! Caretaker. Where are you, you old dog?'

'What do you think?' she says to Andrei, as they clamber over the back wall and drop back into Honan Road.

Andrei mimes some moves with his hands. 'That stuff was amazing. But I don't want to hang around if the Green Hand are here.'

'It was weird he knew so much about us.'

The Russian boy pulls a face. 'But he watching us. And Fei so loud he hear everything.'

Ruby nods. Voice like a foghorn, Mister Tang always laughed. 'You're right. If he's working for

Moonface we *should* be careful. Something's not right with Charlie and Fei. I think they're in big trouble.'

And yet – and yet – already she feels she knows him, that she's met Lao Jin somewhere before, maybe years ago.

'Ask everyone you know,' she says at the corner. 'Someone must know where Charlie and Fei are.'

The Russian nods. 'You coming back tomorrow morning then?'

'Maybe,' she murmurs, but already, deep down, knows that she will.

She walks home briskly, any trace of the fever and tiredness forgotten, Jin's quicksilver smile still lingering.

Only now does a thought hit her: she didn't get a chance to grab the Almanac, and so there's no chance of getting another talisman drawn today.

Maybe Yu can remember it well enough? Perhaps it's worth bending the journey home to pass his place. But somehow that need for the spirit protection has eased just a bit. All the time she was talking to Jin it was as good as gone, and even now, bizarrely, it feels like he's still watching her. He laughed about the fox, but he didn't dismiss *me*, she thinks.

Thoughtfully she turns towards Yu's leafy, well-to-do street in the French Concession, the trees turning towards copper and gold around her. The first hint of coolness in the air that will make the humidity of summer disappear like a dream. She's so absorbed that she doesn't spot Mother coming down some steps near Rue du Consulat, and nearly bumps straight into her.

Mrs Harkner has just left a terraced house, her eyes smudged and red, and seems so lost in *her* own thoughts that she doesn't recognize Ruby for a moment.

Mother looks unusually flustered, like a bolting pony at the races. 'I am most sorry, I—

'It's me,' Ruby says, dismayed to have been caught out, bracing herself for a scolding and the inevitable punishment.

Mother's mouth opens in surprise. Her eyes flick from Ruby to the house and back again. 'Ah – there you are. Right.' With a handkerchief she takes a quick dab at her eyes and then seems to see Ruby properly. 'What on earth are you doing up? You're supposed to be in bed.' She grabs Ruby's hand and tugs her down the street. 'When we get home I'm going to get Father to read you the Riot Act!'

Ruby wriggles her hand free irritably. 'You're hurting!' It's a street she doesn't know well, and this house has never figured in any of their boring trips socialising with 'nice' girls from Saint Joseph's. Her eyes search for the door that Mother has left in such a state. Number 354. There's a small brass plate next to the doorbell, but she can't make it out. In the front window an antique chandelier hangs, a dozen or so white candles burning.

'What are you doing here?' Ruby asks, planting her feet.

'Just a friend,' Mother murmurs, taking hold again and towing her towards a waiting rickshaw. 'And you're in no position to ask anything.'

As Mother tugs her away Ruby just manages to read the name at the corner.

Red Flower Street. Why is that familiar?

The journey home is heavy with unspoken words. Every now and then Mother's breathing catches. Her face is screwed tight, but it's more distracted than angry when Ruby dares a peek at it. The two times she opens her mouth to try and explain, Mother looks at her almost as if surprised to see her on the seat.

And yet, as Riverside Mansions swings into view across the Wilderness, and the happy family on the Shanghai Dairy hoarding beam their frozen smiles, Mother takes her hand and, instead of delivering a slap like she does when really losing control, just squeezes it gently for what seems like an age.

'We care very much Ruby. We just want what's best for you.'

Is she crying? It certainly feels like it, a soft tremor coming down Mother's arm though the white glove. Bewildered, Ruby sits there, eyes fixed ahead, braced, wondering where Charlie can be, wondering why she can still sense that stranger's energy and ease hovering over her. Wondering what waits in the flat.

She only half listens to the lecture from Father, her eyes roving the hallway, the mirror, wondering if it feels colder in the living room.

And even Dad seems to be only half interested as he repeats all the dangers she faces from *disease, vagabonds, undesirables*, all the things that they as parents are doing for her, the difficulties they all face, the importance of being *responsible*. Amah watches from the kitchen door, waiting for a chance to flash Ruby a smile in support.

'You went against strict orders,' Father says, preparing to pronounce sentence. 'So you are *forbidden* to see those Tang children until at least a week back into term. There are plenty of girls at school you can have as friends. And we need to be sure that you're better too. We all know how fast things can change . . .'

His voice breaks off as he looks at Mother.

'Where did you say you found her?'

'Ferguson Road. Lost,' Mother mutters, turning around to leave the sitting room, brushing past Amah without a word about her eavesdropping.

'But I *wasn't* lost—'

Ruby's eyes slip to the city spread out below the Mansions, as the last of Father's lecture washes over her. I'm a disappointment, she thinks. I'm Wednesday's child, *full of woe,* after all, she thought, like Mother always said. We all know that. Rather than Thursday's child with *far to go.* And now I'm confined to the flat, and there's no way to get another talisman. *No* way to find out about Charlie and Fei. And no way to get back to the temple and Lao Jin.

The evening is drawing a heavy blanket of sky across the city and even the neon seems paler than normal.

第十三章

THE THING IN THE BEDROOM

Half an hour later she's been banished to bed, relieved that people have stopped listing her failings, glad of the quiet to think things through.

If only I was really Chinese, she thinks, and people didn't think I was a foreign devil, I could spend all day with the Tangs, and maybe one day, when Charlie and I are a bit older, we could just be together.

Somehow . . .

She lets her imagination play with the idea for a while, picturing an alleyway house somewhere on the outskirts. She knows it's fanciful, impossible, but she lingers on the thoughts, wanting to push everything else away for a few minutes. I could get a job. Maybe I could be a reporter like Charlie's dad, she thinks, and travel upriver and bash out articles about the country for English papers and make them see what's really going on. The real China. Or I could learn to fly a mail plane deep into the Interior and see all those places I've always wanted to see and report home again like one of those female aviators in the newsreel. Or do both!

But a foreign woman could never marry a Chinese man. It's out of the question. Absolutely taboo. And if you had children? Mother always says half-castes are right at the bottom in Shanghai, below even the White Russians, lives blighted from day one.

Her eyelids weigh heavily, but she doesn't want to let her guard down, not yet. She opens them wide again, straining against tiredness – trying to spin the fantasy life out just a bit longer and stave off the sleep and the long empty hours ahead . . .

. . . that stalk her . . .

. . . and creep closer . . .

. . . and then at last wrap her up tight.

Bang!

She's wide awake.

God, something's in here! Something's in the room!

Panic constricts her chest. Her heart's going like the clappers and her whole body heavy, like it weighs a ton.

What's going on? What is it?

Every single fibre is shouting that danger is very close by. She struggles to sit up, but the weight on her chest is too much and she barely manages to lift her head off the pillow.

She opens her mouth, tries to scream: nothing comes a half-strangled moan.

Not a dream, she can tell that. I'm awake and this is real. And then in the faint glow from the alarm clock's luminous hands she sees the *thing*.

It's a black presence, blacker than any black she's ever seen, a nothingness stamped in the darkness of the room. About the height of a man, moving towards the foot of her bed. She makes frantic movements with arms and legs, trying to squirm away but it's hopeless, and now the thing is growing, looming like one of those close ups in the picture house, cold and heavy and emanating *terror*.

'No . . . no,' she murmurs, shaking her head.

But the shape keeps coming, creeping onto the foot of the bed, sickeningly real and right there, right now, moving across the sheets, pressing down her legs. Her chest feels heavier, she can't breathe, a coldness filling her mouth and all those stories from the *Strange Tales* flooding her head of spirits sucking the *ch'i* from travellers in remote inns and leaving them stone dead in the morning. How stupid to lose the talisman! And now this thing is going to take her away to wherever Tom is travelling. Far away, voyaging in one of those shifting coffins in the Otherworld, stopping her mouth up with earth.

Can't . . . breathe!

From nothing an image blooms in her mind. She sees Jin working his *ba gua* skills, all that force that lifted him effortlessly into the air. The smile that followed. The memory boosts her courage and seems to free her just a bit, and with one last effort she manages to wrench herself loose from the mattress, tumbling out of bed in a tangle of arms, sheet, legs. The weight shifts from her lungs as she hits the floor and she pushes out a sound, half scream, half shout.

'Noooo!'

A moment later, the bedroom light flares in its glass shade and Mother is standing in the doorway, one hand to her mouth.

'What in blazes are you doing?'

'I – I,' Ruby gulps, chest heaving, trying to make sense of what has just happened, blood thick in her veins. 'There was something in the room!'

Mother shakes her head. But there's real concern in her eyes mixed with the impatience. 'It was just a dream. A bad dream and nothing more.'

'It wasn't! It was here, a *thing* in the room. It wanted to get me.'

Mother ventures in, arms wrapped tightly.

'It is cold in here. Maybe the air conditioning . . .' Her voice wavers, eyes swivelling around the room, again that wild look flaring her eyes and nostrils.

Ruby follows her gaze. Everything is where it should be, nothing disturbed on the desk, her dark dressing gown hanging on its hook by the door. She sniffs the air, wondering if there's a whiff of fox to be detected. But there's nothing.

She feels Mother's warm hand, cold wedding ring on her forehead.

'Your temperature's not come back. But you need to rest.'

'But—'

'I'll leave the light on.'

'I'm not making it up—'

'Get some sleep.'

As she prepares to close the door, Mother's eyes take another quick sweep around the room, her fingernail tapping away at her teeth in thought.

'There's nothing here,' she mutters, and closes the door.

The room is silent now apart from the thudding of

Ruby's heart. She hears her parents' door close, Dad's voice rumble. The ventilator grille on the far wall is breathing out air quietly, but nothing else comes from it, no bumps or drawn out moans. Overhead the light and its shade hang straight down.

But that sense of presence just won't go.

It was so real, so close. Didn't feel like the fox in the temple, she thinks, not even like the cold breath of air that brushed against me when the wind bells were shaking. This was something else entirely. She pulls the covers around her shoulders, eyes scouring the room, checking and rechecking for anything untoward but can see nothing.

Something is odd though. Every time she recalls that image of Jin she feels a little nudge of courage, a reminder of the Ruby of old, the Ruby that acted on a whim, who relied on instinct and confidence and thrived. She's felt a flicker of it these last few days. But now it I need to be that girl again, she thinks. I need to be Shanghai Ruby and *act*. And whether it's Charlie or the meeting with the mysterious Jin or the pressing need for a new talisman, the first thing she has to do is get out of the Mansions.

Maybe Amah can think up an excuse to take me downtown? No – she loves me, but she values this job too much to risk it. Maybe I could offer to run an errand in the morning? No, they'd see through that like a shot.

The clock keeps ticking, drawing out the minutes as she forms and rejects plan after elaborate plan. Out on the wasteground she can hear a dog barking faintly, a solitary bark every few seconds. Almost like it's asking a question each time and listening for a reply in the gaps between. Her pulse is still bounding, her chest tight, the alarm clock tick tocking, the ventilator grille humming, the air in the room oppressive and the dog outside keeps barking and barking those sharp yaps. Under the covers her legs twitch . . .

. . . and the next moment she's thrown off the covers and is pulling open her wardrobe, hauling out the school satchel from where she gladly buried it at the end of last term. Quickly she packs: a jumper, a pad of writing paper, her pen, half a packet of biscuits that she hid there for midnight snacks.

Just do it, she mutters under her breath. Mustn't think about anything except what I need to do now.

She gets dressed hurriedly, pulling on the faded grey dress that will help her blend into the shadows, black stockings, the old cardigan that Mother told her to throw away but she loves so much. She remembers stories about people running away. Aren't you meant to have a spotted handkerchief? And shouldn't you have a wicked stepmother and be really miserable? Something Ruby does remember: she takes an old blanket from the top of the wardrobe and makes a long body shape, working it under her bedcovers and scrunching up her pyjamas to make a head-sized bundle. She steps back to look at her handiwork. It might fool them for an extra hour or so. And by then I'll have found Charlie, or have a new talisman safe in my pocket.

She takes one last look around, picks up her shoes and lets herself out into the corridor.

To her surprise, voices are still coming from her parents' bedroom. Nothing distinguishable, but the steady drone of Dad's words bumping against Mother's staccato sentences, the pattern Ruby's heard so often since Tom died, but always in the next room, or cut short when she comes in.

What could they possibly be discussing at three in the morning? Well, let them keep their secrets, she thinks. The truth is they don't really care about me. I'm just a nuisance. Ever since Tom died, I've just been in the way. That awful time Mum blurted out, *if only it hadn't been my Monday's child, my golden boy fair of face* . . . and stopped herself short, a shocked look on her face.

That thought helps strangely enough, and she fixes

her mind on it: that she will be actually *doing them a favour* by getting out of their hair. So why not go for good? Run away and start a new life. Andrei seems to manage just fine. The Tangs will help.

And that thought gets her to the front door.

Father's coat is hanging on the stand. Maybe he's still carrying that silver torch, the one he keeps for coming home late across the Wilderness. It would be useful to have that. She reaches down into the deep pocket releasing the scent of aftershave, pipe smoke – and as she does so remembers him standing there at the front door talking to that thin voiced man and the way his hand was thrust there.

She fishes deeper and yes, there's something heavy, wrapped in a piece of cloth. Puzzled by the weight and size, she parts the material and pulls out – in astonishment – a bulky, black revolver. She stares at it, uncomprehending, feeling its cold weight. What on earth is Dad doing walking round with a gun? She knows he brought his service revolver back from the trenches, but even when Tom pressed and pressed to find out about the wound that put the limp in Dad's leg, and nagged to see the gun, it was always kept out of sight, fenced off by a silence and firm shake of the head that left them both wondering. And wary.

Whether or not this is *that* gun she has no idea. Or

why it's ready to hand in his pocket. She just knows it shouldn't be there, part of the Dad she doesn't really know these days.

Need to get rid of it and the danger it carries. Chuck it somewhere.

Without another thought she grabs the stupid thing and buries it at the bottom of her satchel. The main thing is just to act, to get going.

She listens again. The voices have gone silent in the bedroom and she fumbles quickly in the other pocket, her fingers closing round the pocket torch, and then lets herself out as quietly as she can into the deeper hush of the landing.

For a second she hears her parents' voices start up again and trusting they will cover the sound, lets the door click shut. No keys and the deadlock has dropped.

As she drops down the stairwell she hears the pipes gurgling, the generator humming in the basement. There's a big crack in the wall behind her, new plaster already gapped by some slow settling of the building.

The silty ground shifting beneath.

She takes a deep breath, eyes the lobby and sees the concierge slumped at his desk, head rested on folded arms. It would be a disaster if he were to wake up. He'd recognize her at once and buzz the intercom to the flat and that would be that. The lights are dim though at this time of night.

Ruby darts down the last few steps, across the polished floor and pushes through the revolving door. A car is just swinging onto the half moon driveway, lights slashing the front of the building. She turns her head away to cover her face and sees her own silhouette rear up in front of her, grow to a monstrous figure three floors high and then disappear as the shadows reclaim her and she runs, a loaded Webley pistol heavy in her satchel, committed to the night and to the city.

The car's engine rumbles to a stop.

Behind the wheel Woods pauses, then reaches to turn off the headlights as he watches her go. She's got spirit that girl. But what the hell is she up to now? She lied to me this morning and she hasn't a clue what's going on.

He reaches for his coat on the back seat.

Maybe I should wake her parents, he thinks. Or follow her just in case. No, Woodsy. You've got bigger fish to fry. Dangerous fish.

He checks his own gun and steps from the car. There's a slight shake in his hand as he closes the door and glances up into the heavens.

第十四章

OUTLAWS

The city never really sleeps, Ruby knows that. Not fully, but a greater part of it does seem locked in dreams and nightmares now. Bundled up in rags and blankets, beggars are pressed into doorways, huddled against a night that carries the first taste of autumn. At the corner of Rue du Consulat a rickshaw man is slumped on his seat, exhausted by hunger and the miles and miles in his legs. Two Chinese women shivering in beautiful silk cheongsams are trying to rouse him to get a ride home, poking him with an umbrella, laughing as he slumps sideways, sound asleep.

I'll head for the temple, she thinks. Lie low there until it's light and hope Charlie and the others turn up. Copy out the talisman, that's the main thing and hope that wards off the Black Thing – whatever it was. Maybe that was even the 'Terror' Andrei was talking about?

She sets her jaw, and makes her way through the shadowed streets, past the dance hall, a taxi or two rumbling at the kerb, past the shuttered cinema, Fratelli's darkened windows, past a jade-green tram clanking through the night seemingly without a soul on board, its destination blank.

As Ruby turns for Honan Road and the temple, she thinks she hears footsteps behind, and slows her pace, listening hard. There's the muffled sound of a jazzband whumping away in a club nearby, but is that something else? The fine hairs on the back of her neck start rippling in waves again, and she stops dead in her tracks, breathing hard, daring herself to look round. One . . . two . . . three . . .

She spins to find herself looking at a thin dog. It gazes back at her, neon light from the jazz club falling on pale coloured fur. It reminds her instantly of the one in Nantao – but it can't be, can it? Surely the colour's not quite right? Hundreds of stray dogs in this city, all mongrels, inbred and blurring towards that same half-starved look. She waits for it to move away, crouching to pick up a big stone lying in the gutter in case she needs to chase it off. But the dog simply wags its tail and keeps looking at her, panting as if it's just run a distance.

Cautiously it takes a step towards her now, then

another. Rabid dogs probably don't wag their tails, she thinks, holding out her hand.

'Here boy, good boy,' she calls, and the dog sidles up to her, sniffing the air, sniffing Ruby, tongue lolling out before stopping just short. It really *does* look the same: those beetling eyebrows, the same amber eyes.

'Who do you belong to then?' she asks. 'How do you keep finding me?'

The dog wags its tail a bit harder, and looks up into the clouds scudding overhead. Ruby follows the animal's gaze just as a huge moon slides clear, a harvest moon singed with orange. The light sparks the dog's eyes and it sinks onto its haunches, before throwing its head back and letting out a long, ethereal moan. The sound wells up from deep within, and carries a thrilling wildness with it, the hint of a vast unknown world as it falls slowly against the trumpet and pounding drums from the club.

'Shhh! Go on, go home, boy.'

She turns and jogs away and the howling stops abruptly. To her surprise she hears the dog running again, claws clicking the pavement, closing fast on her. Maybe it's going to attack after all? She glances back and sees the pale creature lolloping along, tongue hanging out. She grips the stone tighter, ready to fling it if the dog attacks – but instead it just bowls past her, all its interest in her seemingly gone, charging away into the shadows at speed, intent on something only it can see – or hear.

The darkness cupped inside the temple's crumbling walls seems more intense than she's ever seen it when she reaches White Cloud. The gravestones are just vague bumps and she daren't even look at the well. Maybe that fox is still struggling in the bottle at the bottom – or is crawling along in the Otherworld just beneath her feet right now, thirsting for revenge.

She hurries past, sees the darkness that fills it to the brim, and feels the gun jab her back at the bottom of the satchel. Maybe I should hide it away here and play dumb when I go home, she thinks. *If* I go home! The thought of the reception waiting for her when she does is too much, and she shoves it away. I'll work something out, she thinks. *Mei wenti.* Just keep moving now.

The main hall's ornate roof, protected by guardian dragons, is black against the moonlit clouds above. Will the stranger still be here? Or the others? Maybe even Moonface himself might be hanging round?

A few feet from the steps she sniffs the aroma of incense, and something else wafting on the breeze too. Something's cooking, something that smells really good. She follows the trail, picking her way up the shaky steps and onto the veranda – and nearly stumbles over a body.

It's Andrei, lying on his back as if laid out in a funeral parlour, arms at his sides, his face white and eyes shut. For a moment she remembers seeing Tom lying like that. She and the bearded French doctor had at last managed to dodge their way back through the rioting, past the British consul's burning car and into the compound. Briefly she felt elation at succeeding in her mission and bringing help to her brother. Of saving him. But then saw her white-faced parents and realized she was too late after all . . .

She crouches by Andrei, anxiously reaching out to feel for a pulse – but sees now his chest is rising and falling gently. Just sleeping, but so calmly, and why out here on the veranda? The incense is more pungent now, and looking around she spots seven dots of red light smouldering, the sticks jammed into the matting. They're set out in a pattern that seems familiar. Behind them candles are twinkling beneath the statue of the Jade Emperor.

'Hello? Mister Jin?'

There's no answer. She glances at Andrei again. His face looks so relaxed, almost unfamiliar. Chased from pillar to post by homelessness and poverty, struggling with his own loss, it hasn't looked that way in ages, and she doesn't want to disturb him. His breath catches and he turns his head slightly.

This is the chance to hide the gun. She slips the satchel off and rummages to the bottom, pulling out the revolver, breathing in its smell of metal and oil. Chuck it down the well? That doesn't seem right, and there would be no chance of getting it back if she needs to make it magically appear at home again. She remembers the loose board on the steps. It lifts easily and you can tuck something on the support beam underneath. Andrei sometimes hides the stuff he steals there, she thinks. Quietly she wraps the gun with the handkerchief and eases the broken plank up, reaching in and under, shoving the package into the recess. She drops the board back and glances round. Andrei's still asleep, his head turned away towards the Jade Emperor's fierce gaze.

Straightening up she's startled by a black figure looming over her. For one dreadful instant she sees that menacing spirit from her bedroom again, and her breathing tightens, but then the figure shifts and the moon spills over face and shoulders to reveal Jin. He holds up a finger to his lips and nods at Andrei.

'I don't want him to wake up yet. I want a word with *you* first.'

She gulps back shock. Did Jin see her stashing the

gun away? And would that matter? It feels somehow like it wouldn't, that this strange man would just nod and accept whatever she did. Whatever she tells him.

'Is he alright?' she asks softly in Chinese. 'He looks weird.'

'He had a bad evening,' Jin says. 'I saved him from a bit of trouble. And then I did some healing on him.'

'Healing?'

'I did some work on his *ch'i*.'

'How do you work on someone else's *ch'i*?'

Jin cocks his head on one side, considering. 'If I show you something, Ruby, can you keep it to yourself? I'd rather people didn't know *everything* about me?'

'Not even Charlie and Fei? Why?'

'I need to be different things to different people. That's how I work.'

'I don't understand.'

'Don't worry. You will.'

He takes off his hat and drops it to the floor and his face changes before her eyes, the smile slipping away, eyes half closing. He alters his posture, softening his knees into a martial arts' stance, and in that stance it seems nothing could shift him from the spot, not a typhoon, not an earthquake, not an armoured train. Nothing.

'This is how we work with *ch'i*,' he mutters. His

scarred hands float up in front of him, then down, then up again as if brushing through air that is becoming thick and resistant. The movement changes as his fingers start to describe circles, shoulders and chest moving with them, repeating gestures that make her think of trees blowing in the wind, or waves rolling out in the deep sea, and she can't pull her gaze from the swaying of those hands, as his feet shuffle the boards, stirring up puffs of dust. And then he's calming them again.

'Now. Watch.'

He turns his palms to face each other and pulses them together as if squashing something between, something that resists his hands' motion and pushes them apart again. He repeats the action over and over until Ruby imagines she sees a faint glow, about the size of a grapefruit, cradled in the empty space between Jin's curved palms and fingers. She gasps.

Jin keeps his focus, working his hands, compressing the shimmery ball more and more, and as he does so it gets brighter, until there's *definitely* something burning there, and then without warning, he takes two quick steps forward and pushes his palms against her belly. An instant warmth fills her abdomen, as if she's just had a bowl of soup and it's heating her up from inside. And more than that: a deep breath throbs up from her belly, lifting and slackening her shoulders, relaxing her jaw. It feels good. A memory of how she used to feel when she was younger – or thinks she used to feel.

Jin steps back, picking his hat from the floor.

'Well?'

Ruby's still looking at his hands, but the glow has gone. Whatever was pulsing there is now inside her, giving renewed energy and strength.

'What – what did you do?'

'Just *ch'i*,' Jin says. 'When you're really good at it you can generate enough to give some away.'

He walks away into the gloom, beyond the reach of the candles, and Ruby scrambles to follow. She's heard about Taoist masters who can make themselves strong by concentrating their own energy, who can break bricks with bare hands or meditate for hours in the falling snow in wet blankets and cook off the damp. They used to play at it when they were pretending to be the *Outlaws of the Marsh*, summoning powers and superhuman strength to fight evil warlords and bandits. But she never thought she'd witness this. Let alone feel it, not even when she was pretending to be Hu San Niang!

'That's incredible,' she splutters as she follows him into the back corridor. 'How do you do that?'

'Just practice,' Jin says. 'Just years and years and

years of practice. Like anything else.'

'I'm not sure I understand what *ch'i* is. I mean not exactly.'

'No one does. You just need to know that when it accumulates sufficiently and moves there is life, and when it stops and disperses there is death. That is enough.'

The smell of cooking is stronger here. It's very dark in the corridor and she fumbles in her cardigan for the torch. Ahead Jin pauses in the doorway, resting one arm on the pillar, and coughs abruptly, long and hard. He spits a ball of phlegm into the dark.

Ruby flicks the torch into life. 'Are you OK?'

Jin doesn't answer for a moment, his head bowed. When his voice does come it sounds briefly thinner, shakier. 'I'm fine, just been fighting something off.' He splutters again, chest wracked, but then straightens, and his words are strong again.

'Let's eat. And have a talk before the others get here.'

'What do you mean?'

'Charlie will be here in an hour or so.'

'How do you know?'

'Because I asked him to come.'

He ushers her into the monk's cell and in the brittle torch beam she sees a pot bubbling on the stove, scraps of wood burning orange in its belly, sees Jin's possessions laid out neatly, and that pale yellow dog curled up fast asleep on the makeshift bed.

If she's surprised at that, she's even more astonished to see the Almanac lying open next to him, its pages splayed to show a big garish woodcut of a fox.

Once, about a year ago, Ruby found her mother reading her diary. She had stupidly written the thing in English – partly because she thought no one would find the key that unlocked its clasp and partly because her written Chinese was so shaky. In it Ruby had poured out everything that was choking her in those bad days after the return from Hankow on the British gunboat: from her anger at her parents' decision to go upriver in the first place to the fury at the doctor for being so slow that day to make his mind up to risk the crowds, from her grumblings about school, to her dreams of becoming a pilot. Even worse, she had confessed to the diary's thin paper her growing feelings for Charlie, drawn a heart and initials, things that made even her freckles blush.

How much Mother read she never really knew. But she never forgets the startled look on her face, how it mirrored her own, how both of them looked so guilty, how cross she felt later when the shock subsided.

There's an echo of that now, like she's been caught out – something she doesn't want strangers to see. And how has he found the hiding place behind the altar?

'What are you doing with the Almanac?'

Jin doesn't seem to hear as he lights a kerosene lamp.

'I prefer the darkness, really. It's softer on the eyes. But if we must have light let's use this rather than that harsh thing you've got.' He points at the book. 'This *yours* is it?'

'We found it last month. We're teaching ourselves—'

'Ha! Dangerous stuff,' Jin says, sitting down next to the dog and looking at the open page.

'How did—'

'Very dangerous to try and teach yourself, Ruby. Half a piece of knowledge can be worse than none. This book needs a teacher to go with it.'

He taps the woodcut of the *hu li jing*. 'Your fox spirit looked like this did it?'

'Yes. Sort of.'

'And you trapped it using the instructions here?'

Ruby nods, clicking off the torch and folding her arms. She feels a bit put out by the interrogation: he shouldn't just dismiss the Almanac. It works!

'Then you were rather lucky – and a bit foolish.'

'I thought you didn't believe in foxes,' Ruby says, her eyes moving from the book to the dog curled on the bed. It *is* the same one, she's sure of it now.

'Did I say that?' Jin smiles, mock puzzlement on his face. 'Maybe it was best at that moment. One day one thing, the next day another, everything is changing. So our best policy is to be flexible, keep possibility alive. *Right* now, at this moment, I believe you. I believe there are spirits stalking this city, this country. We need to know how to deal with them, the *right* way. All our actions will get reported to the Jade Emperor soon enough.'

Ruby's eyes are still fixed on the dog.

'Is he yours?'

'He follows me. Or the other way around! Can't shake him so I call him Little Brother sometimes. But his name tag said Straw.'

'Could I have seen him in Nantao?'

Jin shrugs. 'Maybe. He does his own thing sometimes.'

An idea strikes her. 'Were you in Nantao the other day? When there was all that trouble?'

Jin looks at her.

'Trouble? We're surrounded by it, Ruby. Trouble in this world and trouble in the Otherworld. And all of it's focussing on this city. Right here.'

He stamps on the floor and the dog opens his eyes,

ears flicking up. Jin sits down on the bed and ruffles Straw's fur. 'The question is what are you going to do about it?'

'I don't know,' Ruby says. 'I just want things to make sense again. Be like they used to be.'

'It'll never be the *same*,' Jin growls. 'Everything is changing. Life is change – or it's nothing. Only the dead stay the same. What we need to do is to keep our eyes open to the change so we can separate the rotten fruit from the ripe. Know when to act and when to be still.' The lines on his face shadow, a ferocity in his eyes that startles her – and then it's gone as quickly as it came and he smiles again. 'And we need to have some soup.'

'But where do we start?' Ruby says. 'Charlie and Fei are in some awful business I think. And a horrible black thing was in my room and—'

Jin holds up a hand. 'You have what you need to cope. You've always had it, I can see that. And now we're going to get you strong and ready, because you've got a long journey ahead of you.'

Ruby chews her lip, eyes swivelling from sleepy dog, to the crackling fire to the Almanac, and back again to Jin's watchful gaze.

'What kind of journey?'

'One that's unique to you. You'll see.'

She nods. 'It feels like that. I think I've always felt that. But I'm a bit scared.'

'So's just about everyone. It's a matter of what we do with the fear.'

Ruby nods at the book. 'Can you do me a talisman?'

'*Mei wenti.*'

'Will it protect me properly?'

'You just need to name the fear, Ruby. That helps for a start. Remember what the wise man said: when you truly know yourself, you need not fear even a hundred battles.'

第十五章

CHICKEN BLOOD, CHICKEN SOUP

As the soup bubbles on the stove top, Ruby describes the wind bells' ghostly dance, the figure in the mirror, the breathing in the air vent. Then swallowing the fear, she describes waking to find the *thing* at the foot of her bed. How it crawled onto her chest . . .

Jin nods. 'You felt you couldn't breathe, here and here?' he taps his own ribs high up. 'And you felt the weight pressing down? But you couldn't see what it was?'

Ruby nods. 'Yes – that's it! Just like that!'

'We can deal with things like *that*,' he snorts, rummaging in his pack for something, before turning to look at her again. 'Let's be quick about it though. Follow me.'

Back in the main hall the chunk of night sky framed in the doorway seems just a fraction lighter, and Ruby feels a twinge of panic. A new day not far off, bringing reality with it. Oh God, what will Mother and Father do when they find her bedroom empty?

Sort this first, she thinks. The rest can wait. What she has seen Jin do – the *ba gua* moves, the *ch'i* projection – is enough to convince her that this is the person she needs to pay attention to right now. We got the fox but maybe we *were* just lucky she thinks. I need real help. And this strange man with his easy, calm manner is obviously an expert.

In the pre-dawn breeze the candles bleed red wax down their sides as Jin sits cross-legged on the floor and puts a sheet of paper on the matting. He points to a cluster of objects in the gloom behind the altar.

'Pass me that silver bowl. Carefully.'

Ruby picks it up in both hands and sniffs the rich, unpleasant odour wafting off the thick liquid slopping inside.

'What is it?'

'Chicken's blood.'

'Where's the rest of the chicken?'

'In the pot.'

Jin reaches for an inside pocket of his grubby jacket and produces a white-haired brush. He licks the point, then settles himself. 'Now, shhh a minute. I need to be clear as I do this.'

He takes a breath and sits up straight, eyelids half closed. As he does so he seems to grow larger, joints cracking, his head inching towards the painted dragons overhead. His breathing deepens, his face becoming like a mask, or some ancient sculpture. Abruptly he grunts, grabs the brush, dips it in the coagulating liquid and starts to draw a flowing series of red squiggles and lines that drift down the middle of the yellow paper. Far more complex, far faster than what Yu did, moving with certainty and focus, line after line after line until the paper is almost full.

Jin re-dips his brush now and carefully dots in a pattern down the margins.

'What's that?' Ruby whispers, spellbound.

'The seven stars of the Dipper,' Jin mutters. 'Each one is a Starlord, you must have heard of them?'

Ruby nods. 'The ones who come down and find out what we've been doing.' She glances up at the Jade Emperor in the shadows.

'Exactly. Their time of year soon. They'll be here to check up on us all.'

He puts down his brush.

The new talisman is beautiful, the lines powerful but controlled. If anything can protect me then this can, Ruby thinks, eager to have it safe in her pocket. But to her alarm, Jin picks the paper up and puts a corner of it to the nearest candle flame, fire catching.

'No! Don't!'

'Doesn't work otherwise,' Jin says, calmly holding the burning talisman up so that the flames throw crazy shadows across his face. 'Quick. Pass me that other bowl.'

Ruby follows his gaze and sees another dish. She picks it up cautiously.

'Just water,' Jin says, taking it and allowing the ashes from the smouldering paper to crumble and fall bit by bit into the water. As the last fragment of red writing turns to black he drops it into the liquid and stirs it around with his finger.

'Now drink it,' he says quietly. 'Drink it all down and absorb the characters into your body.'

For a moment Ruby hesitates.

'The water is purified. Shanghai Ruby would drink it without another thought.'

She takes the bowl, places the metal against her lips and takes a sip. The water is fresh, but you can taste the ash, like sniffing at a cold bonfire dampened by rain. A piece of the charm brushes her tongue and she swallows it, feeling it flutter in her throat.

'All of it. If you want to be protected.'

She nods and forces the rest down, cold water and ash sloshing in her mouth, swallowed, gone. She puts the bowl on the altar and looks at Jin.

'Should I feel anything?'

'It will do its work very quietly. But you won't be bothered by anything like the black figure. At least for a good while.'

'What was it?' she whispers.

'Hard to say exactly. Something specific for you.'

'I feel cold—'

Away in the courtyard a figure moves at the corner of her vision. Andrei is staggering to his feet, his face puffy from sleep. He yawns and stretches and then sees Ruby, and smiles drowsily.

'What – you doing here? How long have I sleep?'

Jin beckons him over.

'A while. It's time to eat now and start to plan our strategy. The others will be here very soon.'

'What strategy?' Andrei frowns.

'Embrace tiger, return to mountain,' Jin says, peering into the dawn. 'How we're going to face our foe and keep ourselves strong.'

Ruby sips chicken soup from battered tin cups that Jin has conjured from the bottom of his pack. Andrei has wolfed his down, holding out his cup now for more, as if he hasn't eaten properly in days. Which of course he hasn't.

Jin ladles more into both their cups, but seems withdrawn and silent now. He smiles at the pale dog who has come to sniff the pot optimistically.

'You'll get some, Little Brother.'

'What about you?' Ruby murmurs, mouth full.

'I can't eat now,' Jin mumbles. 'Not if my magic is going to work.'

'Magic?' Andrei splutters.

'We made a new talisman,' Ruby blurts. 'Because something hideous came after me.'

'That old fox?'

'No, something else,' Jin says quietly. 'The characters will protect Ruby for now.'

Andrei bumps down his cup. 'What about the rest of us?' But Jin glances away, and shakes his head before promptly getting up and striding out.

'What's so special about you?' Andrei grumps.

Ruby rubs her eyes, stinging with the woodsmoke. 'I think it was just after me—'

She breaks off as she hears a knot of voices in the corridor and looks up to see Jin returning. And following him, with a surge of relief, she sees the slim-shouldered figure of Charlie.

第十六章

COMRADES

In the lamplight his normally healthy face looks pale. Any hint of his quick smile is gone, his forehead and eyes tight with tension and tiredness. An angry scratch jags across his cheek, and he reaches up to it as his gaze swivels from Andrei to Jin to the dog – and finally to Ruby. As he turns his head she sees his spectacles are broken, one lens missing and the arm bound up with twine. She waits for him to speak, to move forward into the room, or even for his face to brighten when he sees her, but Charlie just hunches his shoulders looking dazed.

He glances at Jin. 'What's going on?'

'Where have you been?' Ruby says, taking a half step towards him. 'What's going on with you and Fei? Are you OK?'

Charlie looks back at the stranger, the suspicion

clear on his face. 'What's going on Ruby? I mean it's *four* in the morning and you're both here with this drifter, and—' He stops mid-sentence, puffs out his cheeks and plonks himself down on the bed, bowing his head. 'I'm sorry. I'm just completely whacked.'

There's silence. Straw gets up and stretches, and then goes over to sniff at the newcomer. Charlie reaches out a hand to ruffle the dog's head, but keeps his own lowered, breathing deeply.

'Why aren't you with your dad?' Ruby presses. 'And where's Fei?'

Charlie looks up, a hint of a tear in his eyes, the pressure on him clearly just too much for a moment. He glances again at Jin.

'Who are you?'

'It's OK, Charlie. Your dad and I are on the same side. You have nothing to fear from me.'

'How can I know that?'

'I knew your family – years ago. When your dad and Auntie were small. Peach Blossom Village.'

Charlie leans back, his own curiosity roused.

Jin nods. 'I was much younger then of course!'

'Dad never mentioned your name.'

'I had a different one then. Had to change it.'

Andrei watches from the shadows, straining to understand the quick exchange.

Ruby is trying to hold back now and let Charlie take a moment to regain his composure, but the desire to know what's going on is too much.

'Where's Fei, Charlie? And what were you doing in Nantao when that student was executed—'

Charlie's eyes widen and at last he turns to face her properly. But there's irritation in his eyes, anger snagging his voice. 'How do you know about that? It's nothing to do with you!'

That hurts. She doesn't want to be arguing, but that's not fair. And this isn't how she imagined the reunion going. 'Of course it's got something to do with *me*!'

'You don't know what's going on.'

Jin holds his hands up, like one of the turbaned policemen calming the pounding traffic. 'We're all on the same side here. Let's sit down and talk things through comrades.'

Charlie thumps the makeshift bed with his fist, and then gets up and stalks towards the main hall, muttering under his breath.

Ruby looks at Jin. 'What should I do?'

'Follow him, of course,' Jin says, 'and sort it out quickly. Be honest.'

She finds Charlie sitting in front of the statue of the

Jade Emperor. Through the open door of the hall, carried on the scrap of a breeze, comes the hoot of tugs and faint chanting of the wharf coolies already at work in the docks.

He doesn't look round, but she sees his shoulders soften a bit as she approaches.

'I can't tell you what's going on,' Charlie says bluntly.

'But we've got an oath,' Ruby pleads. 'We're supposed to tell each other *everything*—'

'I've made other promises to other people too . . .'

She takes a breath and then sits down beside him, feels his gaze turn towards her.

'*Our* promises should matter most.'

'How do you know about what happened in Nantao?' he asks.

Ruby chews the truth a second, then spits it out. 'Because I followed you. Because I was *worried* about you!'

'So *you* broke the oath too,' Charlie says. 'And what did you see?'

'I saw you go up to a noodle seller and get some kind of package. Then I followed you through the barrier and into the Chinese City—'

Charlie groans. 'Forget you ever saw that man. OK?'

'And then I got lost and some men chased me, but

I got away and then I ended up in the square and I saw them arrest that poor student and then I saw you. And—'

'What did the men look like?' Charlie says sharply.

'I dunno. Just petty thieves, I suppose. There – I told you. Now you be honest with me. What's going on?'

Charlie sighs and looks away.

'That man – Lao Jin – can do amazing things, Charlie! I saw him make *ch'i* glow in his hands and he wants to help us—'

'We can't trust *anyone*,' Charlie says, getting to his feet. 'What have you told him?'

'Nothing! Because I don't *know* anything!' Ruby cries, exasperated. 'Dad's acting weird, Mum's going to bits again, the temple's been sold to Moonface, and all of that I can cope with. But I need you, Charlie. I need you to be my friend. I can't face it without you.'

The bamboo shuffles restlessly in the courtyard as she waits for Charlie to respond, and its sigh masks Jin's quiet footfall as he comes to stand right beside them.

'She's right, Charlie. She needs you.'

'But all this stuff about ghosts and stuff . . .' Charlie says, shaking his head roughly. 'I'm messed up with *real* danger. I've lost Fei. And I don't know where

Dad is and he could be in real trouble. If he isn't dead already.'

Ruby glances at Jin. 'What do you mean?'

'We had to take that parcel for Dad. It was really important. Then the warlord's men turned up and it was just dreadful. There were Green Hand in the crowd agitating. Fei and I got separated in the crush and I thought she'd been arrested, and I went for a soldier.'

Charlie points at his cheek. 'Bayonet. And then I got away and got a glimpse of Fei near the barrier . . . and I haven't seen her since.'

Lao Jin coughs. 'And what about . . . your dad?'

Charlie peers at him hard through the broken spectacles. 'What about him?'

'I went to your house,' Ruby says cautiously. 'Your dad was there but he was acting really strangely. And he said he was off to Shandong. With you!'

'He's in hiding,' Charlie says, his shoulders sagging again as he gives up the secret. 'He's in a safe house somewhere near the river, but I'm not sure where. He wouldn't tell me in case I tried to follow him and someone was tailing me.'

'But why, Charlie?' Ruby presses gently.

'He wrote an article supporting the Communists. And he's been printing stuff for them. Now he's in trouble with Moonface and his gang. They want him dead.'

A silence falls. Mister Tang, a communist! It doesn't entirely surprise her – not with all his impassioned talk about a better future and equality for all Chinese, for men *and* women. But still . . . the memory of the doomed student and his awful end, the gory stuff in the papers . . .

'One day can be a thousand autumns, comrade,' Jin says quietly.

Charlie looks at him again. He takes his glasses off and fiddles with the broken arm, slim chest struggling against his own emotion. 'Dad said trust no one.'

Jin raises his eyes and glances at Ruby. 'No one, Charlie?'

They both look at her. Feeling self-conscious, she gets up and goes to stand on the veranda, thinking hard. The Communists are meant to be vile creatures, every Westerner and a lot of the Chinese in the Settlement say so – but Mister Tang is a *decent* man. He *listens* when Ruby talks about her dreams of being a pilot or a journalist instead of just laughing.

She knots her arms. 'Then we've got to help him. And we've got to find Fei. We need to get a move on.'

She looks for Lao Jin's reaction and sees Andrei standing just behind him.

158

'What's going on?'

'Fei's missing.' Ruby says. 'And the Green Hand are after Mister Tang.'

'Then he is good as dead—'

Charlie snaps to his feet, eyes flashing. 'Don't say that.'

Andrei shakes his head. 'Stuff like that happens here. Like to my brother. And if I found his killer . . .' He raises two fingers as if aiming a gun, mimes a gunshot.

Lao Jin puts his hand on Charlie's shoulder. 'First we need to make sure Fei is where I think she is. Then we'll get your *baba* to safety. I can ask some friends to help.'

'What friends?' Andrei says. 'I've never seen you in any of the hostels around here before.'

'Really? I thought everyone knew me!' Lao Jin smiles. 'We'll meet back here and I will show you some proper Taoist magic to help you—'

'But this isn't time for messing round,' Charlie groans. 'Dad is in *real* trouble, Ruby—'

Jin stamps hard on the floor, so explosively loud it makes them all jump. One moment he's looking easy, relaxed – and the next, with a tiny movement of the leg, he's made that thunderous sound, his face stern.

'I'm not messing around, young man. We're all in

real trouble, and one of us at least is in more trouble than the rest.' He glances at the graveyard, the stones crouched in the murk of the pre-dawn. His face has taken on that timeless look again, as if he's wearing a mask from the Chinese opera, stern and resolute.

'Moonface is ruthless and his men are *everywhere*. You were all followed into Nantao by his men. And one of them has even been in Riverside Mansions, Ruby.'

'How do you know?' Ruby says, dismayed.

'I have friends – and eyes – everywhere.'

And in that moment she remembers Dad's heated exchange at the front door, the way his hand was groping for the revolver.

第十七章

FIRE BALLOON

Half an hour later Ruby and Charlie are jogging through the streets of the French Concession, the dawn bleeding a weak light overhead. The grand buildings near the river are silent watchers as they scurry through the shadows beneath.

They haven't really spoken since leaving the temple, Jin's last words still loud in their ears. 'Do what I say and then come straight back. Don't trust anyone but each other.'

Ruby glances sideways at Charlie. He's not giving anything away, just a determined grip in his features, as if he's focussing on something over the horizon. He still seems slightly cross with her though. That's worrying. *I only want to help for Heaven's sake,* she thinks, *and he should have told me about his dad, the trouble they're all in.* And she's dying to tell him about what's been happening: about the Black Thing and the new talisman and the *ch'i* . . . But knows she needs to bide her time, wait for the right moment. He won't listen to it right now.

They round a corner and the sprawling Wilderness lies before them, wraiths of mist rising in lines that meander across it. Dad said they were the 'ghosts' of old streams, the ground underneath still that bit wetter and breathing up its dampness, making twisting curtains in the early morning light. He had smiled the first time he saw it from the new flat, a smile like he used to make – maybe the first time he'd smiled properly since Tom's funeral, and she'd been glad to see it. But now the snaking mists look ominous in the half-light. Always the fiercer stray dogs and the crazier beggars who make their homes out here, she thinks, amongst the thistles and stinging nettles and broken down shacks. Dangerous ground at this time of the day.

Charlie looks round, voice edgy. 'Come on!'

She nods and looks ahead, but her courage falters for the first time since she left the flat. There are shadowy figures moving near an old hut, just behind a line of scrubby trees.

'What's the matter?'

'I had trouble again,' she says eyeing the mist.

'There was an awful thing in my bedroom. But Lao Jin's done me a talisman . . .'

Charlie's eyes gaze heavenwards.

'I swear it, Charlie. On our blood oath. On Tom's grave . . .'

Her voice stumbles. She thinks of coffins beneath the ground. She thinks of the day of the funeral and how Mum fell apart so completely at the moment the *ground swallowed him up*.

'Do you think it's safe to go this way?'

'Safer than any other route,' Charlie says. 'The Green Hand don't use it much.' He wrinkles his nose, and then his face softens a bit. 'Most of them don't like getting their shoes muddy.'

He takes off his glasses and turns to Ruby, his eyes searching hers out properly. 'Listen, what do you think of this stranger, Jin? Something doesn't add up at all. He says he's always been round here, but none of us has ever seen him. And he says he knows Dad, but I never heard the old man mention anyone like him. Nor Auntie.'

'But there's something amazing about him, Charlie. Can't you feel that? He did the *ch'i* exercises, like the ones in the Almanac, and it really worked! He made a ball of it about this big and gave it to me.' She holds her hands like Jin held his, imagines she can feel the

163

afterglow of the energy and as she does so it puts fresh confidence into her body, lifting and sparking her eyes. Maybe Charlie sees it reflected there, because he goes to argue – and then checks himself.

'You felt it here?' he says, touching a point just below his belly button. 'In the *tandien*?'

Ruby nods eagerly. 'And we – Andrei and me – saw him do this amazing *ba gua* stuff.'

'Even so, that doesn't mean we should trust him. Even if he *is* a decent martial arts fighter. He might still be working for Moonface. This could be a trap, Ruby. Maybe you should just run on home and leave me to—'

'No!' Ruby's voice is sharp, a pistol shot on the quiet air.

'Keep your voice down!'

'I don't care. The Green Hand don't scare me.'

'Well, you should be scared,' Charlie says. 'A friend of Dad's said there were ten bodies laid out on the mudflats in Soochow Creek last week. They were tied up and shot in the back of the head one after the other. One bullet each.'

The breeze is picking up from the river, moving the mist around them, water droplets thickening, condensing, pulsing.

'I'm staying with you,' Ruby says firmly. 'Until we

164

find Fei and help your dad out of the city. I'm sure we can trust Lao Jin. If he says Fei is with Amah, then she must be with Amah.'

She sets off without a backward look at Charlie, trusting that the force of her words will sway him, pushing through the scrub trees and out across the faint path they always use.

'Wait,' Charlie hisses, and with relief she hears his feet hurrying to catch her. And is even more glad when he adds, 'I'm not sure about that Jin. But I need you to help. If he did see Fei like he says, and sent her to Auntie's place, then I need you to get me in there.'

As they hurry on towards the Mansions the rest of the city is coming back up to wakefulness, the first trams clattering on Deux Republiques, the honk of a car horn, the ringing of a police or ambulance bell haunting the mist. Now she's got Charlie on side, Ruby's thoughts turn towards home.

The tiered white building materialises out of the grey dawn in front of them, a crow motionless and black on top of the Shanghai Dairy sign.

Charlie turns as they reach the last pocket of blackberry bushes, carefully keeping them between him and the driveway. Sparrows are flitting the tangle of branches, wings thrumming the damp air and the fruit are fat and darkly ripe. She remembers eating them with Tom, two years ago it must be. A beautiful autumn day, and we filled that bag with purple blackberries in the sunshine.

'You ought to go in on your own,' Charlie says. 'You live there after all – and the Green Hand won't bother you even if they're around. It's me and Fei they want.'

'But a man came to *our* door . . .' Ruby whispers, crouching down next to him.

'What do you mean?'

She describes the thunderous knocking, Dad's awkwardness, the reach for the gun in his coat pocket. How she picked up the leaflet and had that visit from Woods.

Charlie listens hard, chewing his lip, but his eyes open wide when he hears those last words about the flyer. 'What did you pick it up for?'

'I didn't mean to but—'

'And why hold onto it?' he groans. 'Dad printed them. You're a link back to him. And it sounds like your old man's messed up in something too.'

Ruby shakes her head. 'But he can't be.'

'He works in Customs. They're all on the fiddle,' Charlie sighs. That alarm bell is getting louder and

166

instinctively the two of them crouch lower in the bushes. The fallen overripe berries squidge underfoot, squirting out dark juice and releasing their sweet smell.

'But not Dad . . .' Ruby says quietly. 'He couldn't be mixed up with people like that. Maybe it's just a coincidence—'

There's a squeaking behind them, a knife of a sound in the muffled air, and they both turn to see a figure emerging from the mist. A porter is trundling his long barrow across the bumpy ground, six exhausted female factory workers slumped in rows back to back, eyes clogged by their twelve hour shifts, oblivious to them and everything else. The breeze picks up, sweeping the veils of mist inland towards the heart of Shanghai.

Charlie tugs at his sleeves. 'Anybody could be mixed up in anything,' he says. 'Dad always wanted to write for the movies. But he couldn't just sit around telling silly stories, when . . . when there's so much wrong here.'

'The American – Woods – lives a floor above us. Maybe I could ask him for help. He seemed better than most of them, and he speaks Chinese.'

'An American!' Charlie shakes his head. 'They're even more dodgy than the British. Let's keep him out of it.'

The squeal of the barrow is gone, but the police car or ambulance or whatever's ringing its bell is close by now, clanging insistently. Ruby looks back at Charlie, taking in the pinched, worried face, his wrists sticking out from the jacket arms, his broken spectacles. He looks defeated, all the Tang fire and goodwill lost in anxiety for Fei and for his dad. A sparrow feathers through the branches, flicking drops of water, and then lands on a twig by her head. It sits there for a moment amongst the bobbing leaves and berries, head perfectly still, watching her with one black bead of an eye. Then it lifts up into the murk, pulling her gaze with it. If – *if* – Dad's involved with Moonface and his gang, even if he's just taken some bribe or done someone a favour, she thinks, then he and Mister Tang are going to be on opposite sides. And what then?

Something bright catches her eye, an unsteady twinkle of flame drifting towards them in the grey dawn, from the north, bobbing towards them through the thinning mist. She nudges Charlie.

'What's that.'

Charlie squints through his smashed-up glasses. 'I can't see properly.'

But Ruby can make it out now: a fire lantern, a big white one, flying steadily south east across the Wilderness, coming from the rough direction of White

Cloud and the Settlement and heading towards Nantao. As it passes silently overhead she feels the breeze from the river on her cheek.

Weird, she thinks, it's going against the wind. Must be a different direction up there.

The emergency bell clangs, very close by. Another one.

'An ambulance,' Charlie says, peering through the rust-coloured leaves. 'From the French hospital. And there's a Municipal Police car too. What now?'

On impulse she grabs his hand. 'Whatever happens, Charlie, we're in this together. Remember that angry farmer who chased us across the fields? We always got out of trouble by keeping together . . .'

Charlie glances back and she sees a half-smile lift his face. A flicker of the determination and wiry strength that always used to brighten it.

'I think you scared him more than he scared us.'

He holds her hand for a second. Another . . .

. . . then let's go and nods at the building towering above.

'Go and get Fei and bring her out. It'll look weird if I go in.'

'And then what? Perhaps I should go home. Or maybe we should head back to White Cloud. I want to talk to Jin again—'

'Let's make sure Fei's safe first,' Charlie says decisively. 'Then worry about the rest.'

'Mum and Dad are going to be livid when they find I've been out. They might send me back to England and some God-awful boarding school. They keep threatening to—'

Charlie grins, a genuine smile now that she feels reflected in her own face. 'Fate worse than death, right? In that case you can come and live with us when this is over. Come to Fei's school.'

'I'd like that,' she says, and feels the blood rushing to her cheeks. No more dull British Kings and Queens. No more teasing from those silly Settlement girls about her *beetroot face*, her wild hair, her clumsiness. No more trying and failing to please Mother, to reach out to Dad.

'I'd like that,' she says again. But Charlie's already looking away, back to the scene unfolding at the base of the Mansions, his face grimacing. 'There's another police car. And another. Something's happened to Fei. I know it.'

Ruby straightens up, smoothes her cardigan and dress and sweeps her hands through her damp hair to make it look more respectable. 'If I'm not back in twenty minutes go back to White Cloud and wait for me there.'

Charlie nods. And smiles again in spite of everything. 'You're more like you used to be, Ruby. You know that?'

第十八章

SAD CLOWN

As she walks Ruby picks stray blackberry leaves from her clothes. *Need to look like I'm just a normal Shanghailander girl,* she thinks. *Just been out for a stroll and I've no idea what's going on.* She tries to loosen her arms and swing them a bit, but the nervous energy of the men around the huddle of emergency vehicles is infectious, and her heart starts to bound.

Normally the driveway is kept clear by the concierges who fuss around in their white gloves, moving on hawkers and rickshaws touting for business. But two black police cars are parked haphazardly at the bottom of the entrance steps, and a bulbous ambulance parked between them. The third police car is spilling out two more men who run urgently to the front steps.

Ruby shoves her hands in her cardigan pockets and marches forward.

The daylight is still spectral, a thin sun trying to puncture the mist. A figure detaches itself from one of the cars and comes to block her, reaching out a hand with splayed fingers. One of those uniformed Municipal policemen who look like they've just come from a stint in a prison 'back home', rather than a lifelong Shanghailander.

'Now then, Miss, what are you up to this morning?' He grunts the word 'Miss' in the way that sounds like he'd rather not use it at all.

'Just going home,' Ruby says crisply, trying to hit the tone Mother uses with shopworkers. She's been talking Chinese exclusively all night and it feels odd forming the English words. She tries to ramp her accent up to what Mother calls pish-posh. 'I live on the eighth floor.'

'Just a moment,' the Grunt says. 'Building's shut—'

'What do you mean *shut*?'

'I mean – MISS – that no one is to enter or leave until I say so . . .'

He strolls off towards the lobby, keeping his hand stretched behind him in warning. Ruby glances back to the bushes across the drive, but there's no sign of Charlie. Strange to think of him watching. She ponders making a dash for the entrance, but far better to play the good school girl now.

Another man is coming over, a young officer in a suit, his face set and impassive. 'Sorry, young lady. I'm Detective Sergeant Marwin. We've had some trouble in the building and I've just got to be careful.'

'Trouble?' Ruby parrots, trying to sound vacant, but her pulse jumping again. 'Surely not.'

'Nothing to worry about, but just need to take your name.' He pulls a notebook from his pocket.

'Ruby. Ruby Harkner.'

'And your flat is . . . ?'

'Eight oh nine.'

'And what time did you leave the building?'

She's not expecting that, and feels her eyes widen in panic.

'What – what do you mean?'

Marwin scratches his chin. 'What I say. What time did you go out for your walk? Trouble was on the floor above yours so you might have seen or heard something.'

'Um – about half an hour ago,' she says hastily. That sounds plausible doesn't it?

'I see.' He frowns. 'And where have you been?'

'Just walking near the go-downs on the river.'

'I'm not sure I'd recommend you did that on your own at this hour,' Marwin says, scribbling in his notebook. 'Just hold on a minute, will you?'

He's rumbled me, Ruby thinks. But at least if the

174

trouble's on the ninth floor it's not our flat. Or anything to do with Amah up in the servant's quarters at the top. There's a growing huddle of figures in the lobby now, a concierge opening the main doors – and a moment later two ambulance men struggle out with a stretcher carrying a large body.

With a drag to the stomach Ruby sees a sheet has been pulled right over the face of whoever it is. That means they're dead, she thinks. And it can't just be a heart attack or something or there wouldn't be three police cars. The orderlies are struggling down the steps from the entrance and Marwin has drifted towards them. Instinctively, Ruby follows, her focus, and everyone else's, drawn to the unfortunate soul being carted away.

As the stretcher reaches the tarmac, the sheet slips and somehow a corner of it goes under the shoe of the first orderly. His next step tugs the shroud from the heavy form, whisking it like a magician sweeping away a cloth – and, close now, Ruby gets a long clear look at the face of the corpse.

It's Woods.

Or at least she's pretty sure it's Woods, because something really weird has happened to him. Almost every last shred of colour has been drained from his battered face, leaving blotches of chalk white and pale,

pale pink, marked and drawn by grey shadow. His eyes are shut, his mouth turned down, making him look like some sad, starved clown.

Oh God, the poor man, she thinks, her determination momentarily checked. His face looks deflated somehow, pitifully thinner. He didn't seem a bad sort. It seems ridiculous he could change so quickly from that winking, living person to this . . .

. . . heading for a coffin and the ground.

The crow on the sign behind her *scrawks* loudly.

She pulls her attention back. Seeing that everyone is preoccupied, rushing to cover the face and catch the body that is threatening to topple from the stretcher, she takes her chance and slips into the lobby. One of the concierges opens the door for her absently, his gaze fixed on the scene.

Nobody seems to be paying her any attention – even the lift boy has left his post to press his nose against the glass at the front. After a long half minute, the lift door sighs open and she dodges inside and presses the number ten, holding her breath until the door closes and she feels the machinery tug her skyward.

Her mind flips back to the body on the stretcher. She imagines a gangster pulling a gun on Woods, the deafening explosion, the bullet hitting. Or a knife plunging? But there was no echo of that violence on his features, just that sad, sad look. Surely his face should have been twisted up in pain or surprise? And now she feels her goosebumps rise again as she watches the numbers tick up to her floor, to nine, then on to ten. That memory of the Thing crawling over her returns. Even with Jin's talisman done and burnt and swallowed, she can still feel its echo, and wraps her arms tightly around herself.

The bell rings and the doors open onto the tenth floor. It looks and sounds deserted, and she runs to the small stairwell that leads to the servants' quarters above, taking the steps two at a time and emerging breathless in the cramped corridor that leads to Amah's.

The walls are unpainted here, fresh plaster already veined with fine cracks, and the ceiling's much lower than on the main floors. She jogs the length of the corridor to flat S42 and taps on the door, breathing hard.

There's no answer.

'Amah?'

She knocks louder, the sound echoing as she strains to hear Fei's chatter or Amah's steady, good natured tone.

Nothing. For a moment she thinks the tiny room beyond must be empty, but then hears the click of the lock and next second, Amah is standing there, wrapped in her housecoat, stick-thin legs jutting out below.

Amah looks surprised to see her, a bit embarrassed maybe. Her skin is stretched tight with tiredness, her few remaining teeth visible as she opens her mouth in alarm. Ruby's only been up here once or twice and residents aren't generally encouraged onto the servants' floor.

In her surprise, Amah starts in Pidgin. 'You no belong this floor side, Missee—'

'For Heaven's sake, Amah,' Ruby snaps in Chinese, peering past. 'Speak *Chinese* with me!'

'What are you doing up so early? Are you feeling unwell again?'

'What?' It takes a moment for Ruby to remember the illness. It seems weeks ago now, not just a day. 'I'm fine, thanks, Amah,' she says, softening her tone. 'Where's Fei?'

'Where's Fei?' Amah repeats blankly. 'What do you mean?'

'Isn't she with you?' Ruby says, trying to push past.

'Of course not. There's only just room for me,' Amah grumps. 'I liked the old house on Bubbling Well. I had a decent room there.'

Ruby groans and eases past Amah into the cramped room. A small bed, a chest of drawers, a few clothes hanging over a chair – nothing else, and certainly no

Fei. A small black-and-white photo stands on the drawers, next to Amah's silver hair brush.

'What's going on?'

Ruby looks around the room and puffs out her cheeks trying to still the chattering monkeys in her head.

'Mister Tang's in trouble—'

Amah frowns sharply. 'What's that brother of mine up to now?'

'I don't really know,' Ruby says, 'but someone's after him, and Charlie and Fei got separated. A . . . friend said she was here with you.'

'I haven't seen her for days,' Amah sighs. 'And if you *do* see her tell her she owes me a visit. That girl always makes me smile—'

'Hold on,' Ruby throws her hands up in front of her, trying to order her thoughts. 'You mean you haven't seen her at *all* in the last day or so? She hasn't been here?'

'Not a hair of her.'

Oh God. Does that mean she's just made a big mistake? 'Amah, do you know someone called Lao Jin?'

Amah looks at her blankly, then shakes her head. 'You're not making any sense!'

'He says he knows you. He's some kind of Taoist priest or something. He's turned up at White Cloud. He said he knows Plum Blossom Village.'

'Never heard of him. Is he a drunkard like the *sifu* at New Temple?'

'No, not at all,' Ruby says. 'He can do amazing things . . .' But her voice loses force, and trails away into that background hum of the Mansions. If Fei *isn't* here and Amah hasn't seen her, then maybe – just maybe – Lao Jin lied? Maybe Charlie's right?

Maybe it's a trap.

第十九章

TOM

'Now tell me: what's my brother been up to?' Amah asks, face darkening.

Ruby slumps down on the little bed, ignoring her for a moment, trying to work out the mess in her head. Her eyes fall on the photo: it shows some nondescript village, ramshackle buildings, a few trees smoky in the distance. Two figures stand in the foreground, a young woman and a teenage boy, both staring at the camera, their faces caught somewhere between excitement and suspicion, the young man's eyes intense and bright. Behind them in a semi-circle stand a group of watching villagers, some grinning, some stony faced. The young woman must be Amah, that same cock of the head, same shape of the skull. And the teenage boy? Could that be a young Mister Tang? It really reminds her of Charlie, shoulders slightly hunched, glasses picking up the light.

Amah has followed Ruby's gaze and she reaches over to tap the photo frame.

'Long time ago.'

'It's you and Mister Tang, isn't it?' Ruby says.

Amah nods. 'French photographer came through our old village. The Righteous Fists had just started all their nonsense. Trying to block foreign bullets with their bare hands. That was a bad year. Lots of people in our village died and that's when we came to Shanghai to escape the worst of it.'

'Is that when you found all those bodies in the well . . . ?' The story has always horrified Ruby, Amah telling her how it was *filled to the brim* with the dead. Her eyes flick back to the photograph.

Behind the young Amah a man is turning his head away so it's blurred in the camera's blink. He's standing slightly off to one side of the watching crowd, arms folded, and behind him a chubbier figure walking away with his back to the camera.

'That's right. Troubled times. And look what happened to the Righteous Fists: they all ended up dead, or starving in cages. It's always a mess, always the same,' Amah says, looking down at her. 'And there's been something bad in the Mansions this *morning* – a commotion about an hour ago and I went down to check. Apparently someone was killed on nine. Some Yankee.'

Ruby looks up abruptly, attention snapped from the photo.

'Yes,' Amah nods. 'Killed they say. You and I were right about this place, Ruby. It's nothing but bad luck, bad spirits, bad ground. The sooner we're all out of here the better if you ask me. Weird stuff going on.'

'What do you mean *weird*?'

Ruby stares into her face, skin tingling all over, as Amah nods emphatically. 'First there was the chimes and now this. I've heard about this kind of thing before: apparently there wasn't a drop of blood left in his body.'

Ruby pounds down the service stairs, Amah's words still in her ears.

Not a drop left in his body. What on earth could do that?

The thrum of the generators is always louder here, a low level vibration that you can feel in your bones, but it seems even louder today. Ominous. The lighting for servants is dim, leaving thick pools of shadow at each turn of the stairwell and she has to steel herself to push on down.

She badly wants to get out of the building, to run

back to Charlie who must still be waiting in the bushes. But, despite the returning fear that's threatening to make her limbs stiffen, she *has* to go to Woods' floor and try and find out exactly what's happened. Courage and curiosity are trumping fear – just about. She can feel a trace of Jin's *ch'i* working deep inside, burning there steadily, and she imagines it getting brighter, flowing down to her legs, into her arms, as she bursts from the stairwell onto the ninth floor.

Doors stand open the length of the corridor, people milling around in dressing gowns, shirtsleeves, that way people do when something unusual has happened and residents who have been pretending not to know their neighbours suddenly recognise each other. She pushes forward, slipping between the confused Shanghailanders – hearing snippets of French, English, Pidgin.

'*Mais oui! Il est mort.*'

'I was speaking to the fellow only yesterday—'

'But I thought his name was *Carter*?'

'Told me he was working for American Petroleum.'

'*Il m'a dit qu'il s'appelle Woods!*'

'Lose plenty blood, savvy? All blood.'

'*Es muss Communisten sein—*'

'Dead as a dodo the orderly said . . .'

Nobody notices Ruby as she weaves through the

scrum. Two Municipal policemen are blocking the way, and behind them a man with a camera is lining up a shot of what must be Woods' doorway.

'Go back to your flat, Miss,' one of the policemen says.

Ruby nods, but doesn't move. Her skin's rippling all over now, every hair standing on end, every goosebump standing proud, her mouth dry. The corridor's cold too, really cold. Can't other people feel it?

'Which flat are you from?' the other policeman says. 'Go back home and leave this to us.'

Thwump! The photographer's flash lights everything starkly, chasing shadows down the corridor.

'Have to ask you to move back, Miss—' the first policeman says, reaching out to steer her away, but, spur of the moment, Ruby ducks under his arm and runs to the open doorway. I can face it. I can do it, she thinks. I'm Shanghai Ruby.

The burly photographer looks down at her, fiddling with the flash unit. 'Morning, Sweetheart. Should you be here?'

Ruby ignores him and peers into the room. Several men in long coats are bent over something on the floor, one of them pointing. There's a weird smell that's hard to place. Maybe it's the sulphurous flare of the flashbulb, or something else sharpening the air. She edges forward trying to catch the men's conversation.

'It's a print, I tell you,' one of them growls. 'Must be the killer.'

'Rubbish. It's just a smudge from the wound.'

'But where's the man's blasted blood then? You tell me that.'

They all stop, and look up at Ruby. Their features are lined, drawn with tension. The tallest of them, a man with a gaunt face, gets up. 'What are you doing there?' he snaps. 'This isn't a bloody playground.'

She feels a hand on her shoulder and one of the uniformed men is standing there, making a face. 'Come on.' He steers her back into the corridor.

The photographer winks as Ruby passes him. 'I've seen this a couple of times before,' he whispers. 'Upriver. Spoooooooky stuff—'

The thin-faced man cuts him short. 'Need a shot of that print on the floor, Harry. And you,' he adds looking sternly at Ruby, 'beat it.'

She pushes past the onlookers, desperate now to get away. Whatever has happened there has stamped bewilderment and shock on those hard-bitten policemen. And their type doesn't shock easily. Maybe all this has nothing to do with our stuff, she thinks, but I need to tell Charlie.

Ruby bangs through the service door and down the echoing stairway, eager for the light. For a heartbeat she considers returning to her flat and actually doing what Amah has instructed, to *go home and stay put*, but as soon as she runs with that thought and imagines being back in the stuffiness of her room instead of running back down to Charlie, it's unbearable.

Once, a lifetime ago under a hot Hankow sky, she hesitated, waited just that bit too long. If I'd been quicker that day, she thinks, then maybe Tom would still be alive now. I hesitated and that's what cost the time. Not the French doctor.

Her eyes feel wet, tears welling up from deep inside, blurring her vision. Surprised, she wipes hard at them. Get a grip for Heaven's sake, she thinks, can't start blubbing now. She hurries on down the stairwell past their floor, down and down in the dim lighting, and in the blink of her moistening eyes, thinks – or imagines, or dreams – she sees a small figure running ahead of her in the shadows. It's indistinct, light footed and familiar, a bounce in the step that she followed so often, leading her from one adventure to the next . . . But it's gone as soon as her hand has cleared the salty water from her eyelashes.

'Tom?' she whispers.

She stops, blinks again and peers ahead, but sees nothing but the crack in the wall of the service stairwell. And then hurries on.

第二十章

BITTER RENDEZVOUS

Outside, the sun has melted the mist and you can smell the river with its back taste of salt, sewage and coal smoke.

The ambulance has gone, but the police cars are still parked at the front of the Mansions. Ruby skips down the steps, and walks in the direction of Nanking Road as briskly as she dare without raising suspicion. At the last moment, with a quick glance back over her shoulder, she nips across the road, behind the Sunshine Dairy advert, and pushes through the thistles, under the hoarding's skeletal support, desperate to see if Charlie's still there. Has that been twenty minutes? What if it was a trap and the Green Hand have crept up on him? At least that dreadful shiver on her skin has calmed.

Could that really have been Tom in the stairwell?

Or just her imagination working too hard, too desperately, like Mister Tang said?

She's almost on top of the tangled bushes, when she hears Charlie whistle and looks down to see him crouched low in the damp undergrowth, looking up expectantly with an unvoiced question.

It's painful to see the hope wiped clean when Ruby shakes her head and he realizes Fei isn't with her.

'I'm sorry, Charlie. She's not been there. Amah hasn't seen her at all.'

He swears blackly. 'I told you. I *told* you that drifter at the temple was no good.'

'I still trust him . . .' Ruby says. 'Why would he have given me all that help with the *ch'i* if he wanted to trick us.'

'Then where *is* Fei?'

'Maybe something happened to her on the way here.'

Charlie slumps back into the tangle of the bush. 'And what was all that stuff with the ambulance?'

'A man was killed on the floor above us. The one I told you about.'

'What man?'

'Woods. The American,' Ruby says. 'He looked awful . . .' She takes a sharp in-breath, remembering his face, the feeling in the corridor outside his room.

'Someone said he'd lost all his blood—'

Charlie groans again, his face souring. 'Then it's the Green Hand. They say Moonface gets his men to do it to scare—'

'I don't think *people* could do that,' Ruby says. 'It must have been something else. A hopping vampire or whatever the thing is that's been hanging around the Mansions.'

Charlie rolls his eyes. 'You don't know what these people can do. And we haven't got time for *that* rubbish now. We've got to find Fei.'

'I don't think it's rubbish,' Ruby says quietly, but with an intensity that snags Charlie's attention back. 'Your dad himself told me he saw a ghost once.'

'I can't believe that—'

'He said he saw your mum, Charlie. Outside your house. And I think I just saw Tom in the Mansions. He was there in the corridor, running ahead of me. Or away from me. I don't know . . . but I saw him. Like I can see you now.'

She can feel the tears burning and wipes at them briskly. Mustn't let Charlie see me cry, she thinks, gasping for a breath. I want him to see I'm strong, as strong as I ever was. A girl who can cope with anything. Who could fly a plane far into the Interior . . .

But it's no good. She slumps down amongst the

thistles, oblivious to their prickling jabs, reaching to squeeze the bridge of her nose and pinch off the emotion. The sun's coming stronger now, working clear of the hoarding and she feels its warmth on her cheek. A few late butterflies are dancing white overhead.

'Mum and Dad want him back so badly. They'd rather I'd died not Tom—'

'Don't be silly.'

'I'm just in their way . . . it's the truth.'

And then, along with the glow of the sun, she feels Charlie's hand on her shoulder, a steady reassuring contact that spills the next words from her mouth.

'It was *my* fault, Charlie. It was my *stupid* fault Tom died.'

She sniffs up the stuff running from her nose. 'I should have gone to get the doctor earlier. But I was scared. There was shouting outside and one of the legation cars had been turned over. The consul's wife was screaming and they shot her right there. But I *could* have done it. And when I did go, it was too late . . .'

Charlie doesn't say anything, but just keeps that contact. He's eager to get going, desperate to find his little sister, she knows that, and yet he's holding himself now, waiting.

For me, she thinks. For me. She looks up, setting her jaw again.

'Forget it, let's get going.'

Charlie shakes his head. 'I wasn't there that day,' he says. 'But I know you would have done *anything* to save Tom. You're brave, Ruby. You always were . . .'

'Forget it.'

She wipes her face with her sleeve, looking up as a crow lands on the sign above them, claws scraping the metal. 'If it's spirits that killed Woods, then we definitely need to get Jin to help us. We mustn't waste any more time.'

'Tell you what,' Charlie says, a grim smile flashing on his face, '*I* think it's the Green Hand. *You* think it's spirits and foxes. Between us we've got it covered, right? And whatever it is, the first thing we have to do is find Fei. Deal?'

Ruby nods. 'Deal. But where do we start? Your house?'

'Green Hand have got it staked out. Or at least some traitor watching it for us. The old lady opposite owes them money, so . . .'

'Then we should head back for the temple. We've got no other leads.'

Charlie glances back up at the Mansions. 'What about your folks?'

'I'll worry about that later,' Ruby says.

She takes a last glance up at the overblown building,

the sanitised family on the milk advert and wonders what her parents are doing, if they even know she's out of bed yet. But she can't think about that now so she gets to her feet, turning away and setting off briskly across the sprawl of the waste ground—

The pale dog is standing in her path, blocking her.

Straw's eyes are glistening, his tongue lolling. He looks at her and then barks once, twice, the sound cutting the misty air, before turning and trotting away, his barking giving way to a peculiar, guttural growl.

This time she's pleased, not surprised, to see him. Nothing could really surprise me now, she thinks, and feels herself drawn to follow.

'Come on, Charlie!'

Straw keeps making that odd grumbling sound as he picks his way across the Wilderness, turning his head now and then as if to check they're following, repeating the same three guttural noises over and over.

'Grrrrnnnn. Woooohhhh. Lahhhh. Gennnnnn woooh laiiihhhh. Gennn woh laihhh.'

Gen wo lai.

Surely not? It sounds like he's talking, urging her on. Ruby focuses on the sound, resolving it from a growl into a pattern, and into a rough approximation of Chinese words.

Gen wo lai.

Follow me.

She glances round at Charlie excitedly, and is about to ask if he has heard it too. But then decides against it. Don't push your luck Ruby, she thinks.

'It's Lao Jin's dog! He wants us to follow.'

Charlie hesitates, then speeds up to draw alongside. 'He's just a scrawny old mutt, Ruby.'

'You never heard of sniffer dogs? Maybe he's got a scent.'

Charlie is about to argue back, but seeing the look in Ruby's eyes, closes his mouth tight again.

'We'll see where he wants to take us,' Ruby pants. 'And if that's no good we'll go back to White Cloud and make a new plan.'

If Straw could find her in Nantao, and somehow materialise right in front of her last night, then there's every chance he can lead them to Fei. Charlie raises his eyebrows, but says nothing, and together they set off in pursuit.

The dog weaves through the nettles and rubbish, a pale shadow across the waste ground, waiting for them now and then as if impatient, before jogging on. Each time they get close to him, Ruby calls out encouragingly.

'Good boy. Where are we going then?'

He's stopped making that garbled, mumbling growl

and trots on relentlessly, but as they reach the edge of the Wilderness, he stops and barks twice again.

'Ghhhan! Jinnnnn!'

Ruby smiles. 'He wants us to hurry!'

'How do you know,' Charlie grunts. 'He's probably just after food or something. He's thin enough.'

'No. He wants us to hurry. He's taking us somewhere. Isn't it obvious?'

As soon as they cross into Foochow Road the city bursts back into life around them, the bustle and rush of the morning a shock after the emptiness of the waste ground. Cars, motorbikes, the hammering of trams. The pavements are dense with Chinese businessmen on their way to work, Shanghailanders heading for the big offices on the Bund, a few foreign children being tugged along by their amahs.

Straw runs on through it all, dodging legs and rickshaw wheels. If anything he's speeding up as they cross the busy junction with Honan Road.

'Maybe they've already got Fei,' Charlie puffs, struggling to keep up.

'Then we'll get her back,' Ruby shouts. 'We'll rescue her.'

It's strange, but although she should be feeling tired, if not exhausted, she feels OK. Strong in fact, her legs working hard as she pounds the pavement.

Normally she and Charlie are pretty evenly matched, but now she has to keep waiting for him. Maybe the *ch'i* is still helping, she thinks, convincing herself again it's right to give Jin the benefit of the doubt.

The shops are already busy. They pass familiar landmarks: the Siberian Fur Store, a Persian jewellers, a photographer's booth with photos of people waving from the imagined surface of the moon. It's harder to keep Straw in sight here and for a brief second the dog is nowhere to be seen. Ruby scours the crowded thoroughfare ahead, and then she sees him darting straight across the road, flitting between the bikes and trams. She winces, convinced he will be hit, but no – there he is – heading full speed down Fukien Road, and she and Charlie dodge the traffic, craning their necks to keep him in view as he races northwards towards the Creek.

'Wait a minute,' Charlie hisses. 'Moonface's headquarters are down here. Not far. We can't go that way.'

'But we *must*,' Ruby insists. 'Maybe Fei's there.'

'And what are we going to do? Just stroll in and ask if they've got my sister? I can't let them see me, Ruby. They might use me to get Dad.'

'Then *I'll* go. We mustn't lose Straw.'

About fifty yards beyond the next crossroads there's

a line of black-nosed cars pulled up at the kerb, with those inverted chevrons snarling on their radiator grilles. A gaggle of dark figures are clustered around them, a couple breaking off to run up the steps into a squat, brick building.

She's been past loads of times, but always that big brown edifice on the corner with Kiukiang Road has given her the creeps. All that stuff about Moonface's pocked features looming over you as he whispered your fate and then abandoned you to his grisly, bony-headed henchmen.

'We'll be past it in a flash,' she says. 'Besides we can take the next right and head back for the temple if—'

The words die in her mouth. Straw has come to an abrupt stop and is sitting down on the pavement like an obedient guard dog, peering forwards from under his wiry eyebrows.

There's a quiet moment on the street just then, a lull in the confusion of passers-by and cyclists and clutter. In the silence she hears white banners snap overhead, and then – as if everything's happening in a kind of slowed-down motion – she sees a car come from the other direction and pull up in the middle of the street. From it steps a very familiar figure.

She doesn't recognize him for a moment because her attention is grabbed by the sight of a burly man in a coat jogging down the shadowed entrance steps and extending a hand to the individual getting out of the limousine.

They shake, the chubby man pumping the other's proffered hand.

And, as they head back up the steps and into a splash of clear sunlight, she sees the man in the fur coat is indeed Moonface, that ruffled collar of his pulled up around his neck, his round head bobbing as he talks. As they go into the building he pats the taller man with the limp firmly on the back, and suddenly whips round to look up the street, straight in their direction.

There's no time to move, or hide, and anyway the shock has made her go rigid. Moonface seems to hesitate a fraction of a second, as if maybe he's seen her amidst the shadows – but then his men close in around him and all of them, the visitor, the gangster boss, the bodyguards, sweep into the building and are gone.

Ruby swallows hard, looks at the dog, back at the Green Hand building. Then, anxiously, at Charlie. His jaw has gone slack – like some comedian in the picture house – but there's nothing funny about the look in his eyes.

'What . . .' he says slowly, '. . . what the hell is *your* dad doing with Moonface?'

第二十一章

NO DOGS

Ruby stares back down Fukien Road.

The street's back to normal now, rickshaws joggling along, banners fluttering the breeze, sunlight full. The scene keeps repeating in her head, or at least some kind of after image. And the shadows of the men who folded around Moonface and his visitor seem to hover there. She shuts her eyes up tight and tries to picture exactly what she saw, that image of Dad limping along beside that awful man, wonders if she's losing her grip on reality at last.

Dad has changed over the last year, she knows that, even if it's painful to accept it. That father who used to smile, to do silly conjuring tricks with eggs that sometimes worked and sometimes didn't, who took her and Tom on the roof of the old house and swung his telescope to show them the heavens wheeling overhead, he's gone. He went with Tom somehow. But how has he turned into the kind of person who hangs out with gangsters like Moonface? Who has to reach for a revolver when he answers his own front door? It just doesn't make sense – and there's only one way to find out. Ask him! Without thinking she's already moving towards the brown building.

Charlie tugs her sleeve, holding her back. 'They mustn't spot us, Ruby. Don't you see?'

She looks away from his questioning eyes. 'There must be some kind of explanation. I mean, Moonface does do *some* normal business too, doesn't he? I mean, that's how he keeps in with the Council, right? So I'm going to ask Dad.'

'Wait. What did that man say? The one who came to your door.'

'He sounded angry.'

'But what did he say?

'I can't remember. And anyway, what does it matter? I'll ask Dad what he knows and then I want to go back to Lao Jin and ask him what we should do. To find Fei.'

Charlie's peering through his one good lens at the dog who's still waiting patiently, as if for orders.

'It's all too weird,' he says quietly. 'I mean how did this old boy know to bring us here, right now. He plonked himself down just in time to see your dad arrive . . . and how did he know where to find us on the Wilderness?' He shakes his head. 'It has to be coincidence, right? Logically—'

Straw barks again, loudly, for all the world as if telling Charlie to shut up. Just like that, Ruby thinks. Two sharp barks.

And then his ears prick up, and he stands, listening hard to a sound only he can hear, before pushing off and sprinting down the small, dark side street to their right, back towards the river, blinking in and out of patches of sunlight, in and out of sight. The sound of claws on stone grows fainter and then he's gone, swallowed by a block of shadow.

Charlie's eyes stay fixed on that spot. 'There used to be a dog in Dad's village,' he says. 'An old, thin mongrel. Kind of dirty yellow colour, Dad said, and he and Auntie both loved him. He hung around for ages and they used to feed him when they had food spare. Apparently he used to bark like crazy when the bandits were coming to town, or the local warlord was snatching people for his army. A whole hour beforehand sometimes and it gave them time to get away into the countryside and hide. Somehow he always knew they were coming. That's how Dad and Auntie escaped the massacre . . .'

'Maybe it's the same dog,' Ruby says excitedly.

'Don't be daft. That was a long way away. And *years* ago,' Charlie says. 'Let's get out of here. Go back to the temple and see what this Jin of yours has to say.'

Ruby shakes her head. 'I'm staying here. This is the best lead we've got. I'll ask Dad when he comes out. See if he knows anything.'

'He won't let you go. And we're wasting time. Maybe we should have followed your dog.'

'We'll give it a few minutes,' Ruby says. 'And then get back to White Cloud.'

The sun edges higher and Ruby keeps her eyes trained on the building, absently tapping her teeth with a fingernail.

A solitary bodyguard is lounging on the steps, puffing smoke and flicking his eyes up and down the street, but they're tucked in shadow and there's no risk of him spotting them. Every now and then Ruby glances down the side street where Straw disappeared. There's a kind of cool, damp breeze drifting from it, rubbing against her arms, tingling that side of her neck. Must be coming from the river, she thinks, the mist will clear there last.

Charlie is locked in his own thoughts, his eyes glancing from Ruby to the front of the forbidding building. Its upper windows are blinded with whitewash. In big character lettering on the wall the place declares itself to be: MUTUAL LOAN SOCIETY. Ruby screws her eyes up, trying to see through the downstairs windows but it's nothing but shadow inside.

Maybe Dad *is* just on business here, stuff to do with his work in customs. She glances at her watch. Seven forty-five – that's ridiculously early even for Dad to be at work.

What will I say to him? she thinks. The other day, after she surprised him at the front door, there was a moment when she could see that more familiar version of him, accessible, easy going. But she's gone expressly against orders and that's something he's never excused. And if he and Mister Tang are on opposite sides, then that'll be doom for Charlie and her. She'll be on the first boat out, bound for England. She reaches to tap her front teeth again and realises she's copying that habit of Mum's, and pulls her finger away.

Don't think about it.

'What was his name, Charlie?'

'Who?'

'That dog in the village?'

'No idea,' Charlie says, straining to keep watch

on the steps going up to the Mutual Loan Society entrance.

'Just wondering.'

Across from them, a bit closer to the corner, is a European-style café. You can see iced cakes and pastries being piled in the window, and prompted by the sight, Ruby suddenly feels the hunger dragging at her stomach.

She nudges Charlie and points. 'We could go across there. Get something to eat and still be able to see the front. If we sit in the window.'

'Not my kind of place,' he sniffs, casting a quick look at it. 'You never know.'

'It'll be fine, come on. I'm starving.'

'Don't say that. There are people *really* starving around us.'

'It was just a—'

'I know,' he holds up his hand in apology. 'I'm just worried. And dog tired.'

'Me too.'

They're only just over the threshold of the Café Renard when the sour-faced woman on the counter ushers them towards the back of the long, wood-panelled room with a quick shooing motion, her eyes fixed on Charlie.

'I want to sit in the window,' Ruby says loudly in

English, trying to hit that pish-posh note.

'No,' the woman shakes her head, 'those tables are reserved. At the back please.'

Ruby's eyes blaze. It's that ridiculous business of keeping good seats for the foreign residents, nothing to do with tables being reserved. How dare this woman try to stop her friend from sitting where he wants!

'Rubbish, you've got no customers.'

Charlie turns and heads for the door. 'Come on, let's forget it.'

Ruby switches back to Chinese, pulling Charlie towards the tables at the front by his elbow. 'This is *your* country, as much as mine or hers.'

'We shouldn't make a fuss right now. Say I'm your houseboy.'

'No way,' Ruby snaps, then turns to the café woman, flicking back to English. 'We're sitting here. Sit down, Charlie, for God's sake.'

He rolls his eyes, imploring Ruby to drop it, his face colouring. 'Not now.'

It's like the time, years ago, when Amah took them all to the park on the river. A spring day, the river sparkling, one of those days you could believe green dolphins really did grace its waters, but the day forever shadowed by the sign at the entrance to the park stating that the place was for 'Foreign Residents and their servants only'. Ruby had hesitated, while Amah had whispered something to the Tangs. Charlie glowered at the board, gave one of the posts a kick, then let his shoulders drop and mooched away. Ruby had chased after him and told him to ignore the notice, but the day had been ruined.

Incensed, forgetting everything else, Ruby plops down on one of the café chairs, pulling Charlie onto another. He's trying to keep his eyes on Moonface's building, but the café woman's on them now, flapping her hands like a chicken beating its wings.

'At the back. Chinks at the back!'

That does it. Ruby stands up again, looking the woman full in the face. 'You have NO right, you silly woman. This is HIS country. Not yours. If you don't like him then clear off back to wherever you stupid well came from.' The words have backed up for ages, words she's wanted to throw at Mum's stuck-up friends, the men from the club who Dad brings home once in a blue moon. And don't call him a "chink".'

'Get out!' the woman hisses, reaching for Charlie's collar and scragging it. 'And take your dirty houseboy with you.'

Ruby's hands suddenly feel hot, burn with energy, tingle. She brings them swiftly together, feels *something* between them. Turning them palms out, she pushes hard on the woman's stomach, slightly upward, her body flowing with the movement, footwork perfectly timed – and the café owner goes flying back, her face astonished, a full ten paces of flailing arms and tripping feet as she tries to recover her balance before sprawling amongst the tables and chairs.

Charlie's mouth has dropped open.

But Ruby's staring at her hands. Didn't mean to do it that hard, she thinks. Just push her away a bit.

'I'm sorry, I—'

The woman is scrambling to her feet, shrieking. 'What the hell do you think you're playing at, you little brat? Police! Help!'

'Run!' Charlie snaps.

The woman's on them now, trying to grab hold of Ruby, getting a handful of hair and yanking it. Charlie pulls her off, that wiry strength of his always surprising, and spins the woman away, before shoving Ruby down the steps onto the pavement. But the café owner isn't put off easily. She chases out behind them, brandishing a rolled umbrella, swiping the air wildly as she tries to land blow after blow on Charlie's head, screeching.

'Police!'

Charlie wards off the attack; but looking up the street, Ruby sees the Green Hand man turning in their direction. Damn it! He takes a few steps towards them, tossing his cigarette into the gutter, peering at them, a thin, grey, menacing shape in the early autumn sunshine.

Charlie has snatched the umbrella from the woman and is shouting something filthy at her in street Chinese about foreigners and what they can do with themselves, while she attempts to get hold of him by his jacket and drag him back into the café. She catches sight of the Green Hand man and raises her voice, shouting in Pidgin. 'Fetchee police, chop chop!'

The Green Hand man hesitates, then turns and calls out to the building. He is joined at the double by a chubby gangster in a Trilby. They come jogging towards the scuffle on the pavement, half a grin on each of their faces, preparing to have some fun with the irate café woman, and a couple of street kids. Then his face changes. He thumps the other man on the chest and sprints towards them.

And Ruby recognizes them at the same moment: the two men who chased her in the streets of Nantao.

'Bloody hell,' Charlie mutters, 'now we're done for.'

Ruby turns around wildly to look for the best escape route, and far down that shadowed side street she 'sees' Straw quite clearly. Not as if he's standing there, but as if the image in her head and the one she's seeing are superimposed. He's waiting for them, looking their way – and bent over him, stroking his straggly fur, is a small figure.

Tom.

Definitely Tom, lit bright and clear like in the photographer's studio where you stand against the cardboard scenes of the pyramids or inside flying machines.

Her little brother looks in her direction . . .

'Tom . . .' she murmurs and tugs Charlie's sleeve. 'We need to go this way.'

But Charlie doesn't respond, and she pulls him again to follow. Still he doesn't move or speak. And the foul-mouthed woman has gone quiet too. Puzzled, Ruby turns to look back. Charlie's mouth is gaped wide, as if locked in mid-shout, and the woman's waving hair floats motionless in the air. No, not quite – it's moving very slowly as she turns her head bit by slow bit. Time seems to drag, the men on the street make no real progress, their limbs moving as if the air around them has turned to treacle. The first man's hat has come off in his dash towards them and it looks like it's *floating*. Ruby looks round, struggling to work out what's going on, and sees the big clock on the wall just inside the café door, its second hand holding way, way too long on each black blob, a stillness in each slowed and drawn-out second. Bewildered, she turns back to where she 'saw' Tom – and, yes, he's still there, stroking the dog's neck, still looking her way. He looks fine, just like he did the day of the fishing trip, making her laugh and oblivious to what was flowing steadily towards them.

And now it's as if he sees her, because he smiles, and raises his hand to beckon her over. So close, and yet somehow like he's miles and miles away at the same time. Thousands of miles away. A million.

A weird nausea runs through her, and makes her shudder. And then is gone.

'Come on, Charlie, we've got to get down that street.'

Still her friend doesn't seem to react, and then he turns very, very slowly towards her, eyebrows lifting snail pace over the rims of his spectacles as he sees the men closing and the flash of green in the lining of the slow-falling hat. Still it hasn't hit the ground, and even though the men are almost on them, they haven't yet blocked the route to Tom and the dog.

'Time to go,' Ruby shouts, taking hold of his jacket and practically throwing him across the street. 'Get a move on. Follow Straw!'

But that image is fading now. Tom is still beckoning, smiling, and the dog is still wagging its tail on the cobbles, but the clarity and brightness are dimming fast.

There's a rush of sound like the roar of a huge wave breaking. Charlie stumbles back to full speed, everything rushing back into motion, the men chasing them, the woman shrieking, the rumble of a lorry thundering down Fukien Street.

'Run!' Ruby shouts, and sprints away up the sidestreet towards wherever the pale dog and Tom have disappeared. She glances back to make sure Charlie is up and following and is just in time to see the thinner gangster pull a long-barrelled revolver from his jacket.

第二十二章

GREEN DOOR

Inside the Mutual Loan Society building Ruby's dad sits uncomfortably in a stiff-backed chair opposite the pocked features of Moonface. Hovering like a scrawny vulture at his shoulder, One Ball Lu – the gangster's feared second in command – casts a thin shadow on the papers on the desk. When he smiles it looks like his mouth is crammed too full of teeth.

Victor Harkner stares back at the documents.

He wants the whole business to be done, to get back to Stella and make sure she's had a good sleeping-pill sleep and is calmer, and the nerves and all that other stuff aren't about to push her into hospital again. And to make sure Ruby is fine and tucked up safely in bed. Then try and forget all of this, maybe start looking at a new posting. Or even that trip back home at last. It can't be helped, he thinks. What I've done, I've done.

Casualties of war. He adjusts his leg, trying to get the thing comfortable. Weird how you can feel pain in a part of you that isn't even there. He leans forward and taps the paper.

'I've done what you wanted. You've found the girl. Now how about signing this thing?'

Moonface leans forward, the sun blunted through the whitewashed windows picking out the ravages of some old illness, the jowls that still somehow speak of hunger and suffering.

'Maybe. But maybe we wait for results,' the Green Hand boss says in slow, careful English. 'These Communists are tricky. We need them out of the way and we know enough of the Council agrees to our methods—'

'You promised the girl would be returned unharmed. And we *have* a deal—'

'We wait!'

Moonface brings his heavy fist down on the desk with a smack, the fur collar of his coat shaking. 'You go home, Mister Harkner, to your lovely family and wait for instructions. Things are going to get lively on the streets later. Time for us *all* to lay low.'

'But damn it . . .'

Victor's voice trails off as he considers his options. There really had been no choice, he thinks. This is the least worst option, for Stella, for me, for Ruby. There's something about Moonface that unsettles so much, he thinks. Is it the face, the coat? A weird smell about him that you just can't place but seems to take up the air in the room.

'But you must return the girl as soon as you have the father,' he says, getting to his feet.

One Ball Lu coughs and ushers him silently to the door. Just audible in the stillness comes the crack of a distant gunshot. Moonface looks up from the desk, his forehead wrinkling, moist tongue poised between his lips.

Ruby, running for her life, doesn't hear the first gun shot.

Charlie's two or three paces ahead, running hard, and she's just about caught him when something zips past her head and rips a chunk out of the brickwork to her right. The bang that comes with it echoes in the tight alleyway and she spins to see the first gangster not far behind, and taking aim again.

A crazy thought has entered her head, prompted by that feeling of the *ch'i* in her hands, of how that push she gave the café woman felt so strong. She *flew* backwards! Flew! Maybe I should stand and fight? The gun thunders again, its bullet burning a hole in a banner just over her head, making it dance like a pantomime ghost.

Maybe not.

She turns, dashing after Charlie, trying to simultaneously weave and make herself a smaller target. Another alley crosses this one a dozen paces further on and she glances down it . . .

. . . and faintly she sees Tom again. He's about thirty paces away now, running full pelt, turning to check over his shoulder, Straw bounding beside him.

'This way,' she shouts to Charlie, cutting right, following her brother.

'No!' Charlie calls. 'That's a dead end.'

But Ruby's so certain that something extraordinary is happening, that she doesn't so much as break stride. Tom's disappeared again, but she can sense him running ahead, imagine – or just hear – the sound of his feet and the dog's claws.

There's another gunshot and she hears Charlie gasp behind her, his feet stutter.

Oh God, he's been hit, she thinks, fearing the worst, turning as she runs. But what she sees sends an even bigger shock through her body. Charlie's still up and running, his mouth open as he grabs for air – but his face has gone *completely* white, his eyes wide, wide open.

'What is it?' she pants.

'Nothing. Keep – going.'

This alleyway is narrower, lined with firmly closed doors and shuttered windows. It seems to be running to nothing, straight into a brick wall that seals off the street. The footsteps of the two Green Hand thugs are close behind, one of them shouting, his words indistinct, lost in the chase.

'Told you,' Charlie gasps, his feet slowing. His face is still drained of blood and he's looking frantically from one door to another, trying to spot a way out.

Make for the green door.

It's a Chinese voice, whispering softly in Ruby's ear, seemingly coming from no one and nowhere. Very familiar though – and not Charlie.

Embrace the tiger, Ruby. Return to the mountain.

Now she sees it: tucked in the left-hand corner where the dead-end wall meets the buildings, there is indeed a dark green door. It's ornately carved, topped with a scrolling arch – and it's cracked very slightly open. With renewed energy she sprints for it, hoping to Heaven that Charlie is following. That the men are reloading or are far enough behind to give them time to get through it.

'This way,' she shouts, barging across the threshold, her heart beating fit to burst.

Beyond is a courtyard, open to the sky above. No way out but a padlocked door on the far side. The ground is compacted earth. The whole place feels damp and cold and overhead the clouds have gathered, muddy brown. The temperature drops as rain starts to fall. Charlie nearly runs straight into her back, then turns to try and bolt the old door. The rusty mechanism crumbles orange dust into his hands and dissolves.

'Now what?'

'I don't know,' Ruby says, starting towards the door opposite, electric currents chasing patterns across her skin.

And then she sees the figure to her left.

Lao Jin has a grim smile on his face as he detaches from the charcoal shadows. He nods in greeting, carefully turning the sleeves of his jacket back to reveal those strong, sinewy wrists, the calloused hands. He doesn't seem at all surprised to see them.

And Ruby realizes she isn't that surprised either. That's the way this city works. It throws people together, pushes worlds against each other and makes weird things happen that wouldn't happen anywhere else. It dazzles and scares and confuses, and makes entrances and exits as dramatic as the street puppets shoved up or snatched away through a stage floor. It's magical. She always knew it was.

'You took your time,' Lao Jin growls. 'Get behind me. Quickly.'

'There are two Green Hand after us,' Charlie pants, trying to look less bewildered than he actually is. Still that white shock plastered on his face.

'Hats? Or thin ones with green palms?'

'Hats,' Ruby says.

Jin nods, ushering them behind him as the footsteps pound closer. The whole air around them has changed with the rain and it spatters down on them, pocking the mud packed floor of the courtyard.

'Have you got a gun?' Charlie asks Jin.

'What would I want with one of those?'

There's a terrible wait of a few more seconds as the cold rain falls on Ruby's face, darkening Charlie's jacket as each drop hits.

She looks around, wondering if they should take better cover, half a hope she might see Tom again, wondering if the dog was really there, or only in her imagination and now far away.

'What happened to Straw?' she whispers to herself.

Jin glances at her. 'Little Brother's gone ahead—'

'Trapped like rats.' A leering voice cuts him short and they turn to see the two Green Hand men framed in the doorway. They both have revolvers drawn, advancing cockily into the courtyard.

'Drop them here,' the chubby one says.

'Not a bad idea,' the taller one laughs. 'We need to take this little communist alive though. And the foreign devil.' He turns to Jin. 'What are you doing here, you dog? You're meant to be at the temple.'

'I'm here to protect these two,' Jin says. 'Turn around and leave, or face the consequences.'

'A drunken caretaker?' Tall Green laughs, then spits on the ground, cocking the gun and walking towards Jin, training it at his head. The rain is getting harder, but again Ruby has that sensation that time is slowing, details becoming pin sharp all around. She sees – quite clearly sees *and* hears – a drop of rain strike the hot gun barrel and sizzle off in a puff of steam. She can smell the gunpowder still hovering in its black bore and hears Jin move slightly, his clothes rustling as he relaxes shoulders, knees, arms, hands.

'You old good for nothing,' Tall says. 'You're totally expendable and you're in our way. I told One Ball you were a waste of time. And you can't witness this, so very sorry but—'

About ten paces from Jin he fires.

Ruby flinches, but still she sees the gun jump, and Jin's hand fly up and twitch, and brick dust puff behind where the bullet hits. She waits for the blood to flow or Jin to stumble and fall, but he stands there resolutely, facing down Tall.

'You have made people suffer,' he says calmly. 'Now it's your turn.'

Tall aims and fires again – but again Jin's hand flashes and this time the bullet strikes a wall to the side.

'You're a hopeless shot,' the second man growls, shoving Tall Green away, but is only halfway towards aiming his own revolver when Jin moves. He's like a snake striking for prey, dropping low, then jumping through the air, straight down on the man's arm, the gun flying loose, clattering to the ground. Before Jin's even touched the earth himself his right hand has come crunching down on the man's neck, felling him. Chubby lies on the ground, eyes glazed, rain pelting his face.

With horror Ruby sees the taller man, aiming again. He can't miss this time – and Jin's got his back to him. She opens her mouth to warn, but she's too slow and the gun barks again.

As if he has eyes in the back of his head, Lao Jin ducks, and the bullet strikes the wall on the far side, missing by a fraction. He wheels on the spot, arms spread like an eagle and then crosses his hands, catching the Green Hand man at the throat, lifting him clean off his feet and hurling him across the bare courtyard. He slams into the wall and slumps, arms and legs tangled.

There's silence then apart from the sound of the rain.

Jin stays crouched, alert, and then slowly relaxes. He straightens his jacket, then walks loose limbed and rolling, like someone casually stepping from a warm bath, and picks up the two revolvers. There's an old well in the corner of the yard and he steps over to it and drops the weapons in, glancing at the bodies of the two men as he does so.

'If they do come round, they won't find those in a hurry . . .'

Charlie has slumped to a squatting position, gazing at Jin in wonder.

'How could they miss you?'

Jin strolls over, a smile flickering. He holds out his right hand and shows Charlie two bright red marks amongst the callouses on his palm.

'They didn't.'

'That's impossible,' Charlie says. 'People can't block bullets.'

'I didn't. I deflected them. Different altogether. You have to get the timing *just* right and divert the bullet's energy.'

'That's impossible . . .' Charlie mutters again, but

much more quietly.

Ruby peers at the marks on the scarred hand, then looks up into Jin's face, shadowy and mysterious under the battered old hat. She thinks of the Righteous Fists and their belief they could do just this. 'Who are you, Mister Jin? Really?'

He straightens up, tipping his head back to let the rain fall on his weathered face. 'Just an old fighter who wants to put things right.'

'So you're not working for Moonface?' Charlie asks.

'Him and me go a long way back,' Jin says. 'And I'm here to deal with him once and for all. Or help someone else do it.'

He looks back at Ruby and Charlie and shakes himself, like a dog getting out of water, the movement sending droplets flying from him. Charlie is still staring at the red-marked hand as Jin points back to the ornate doorway.

'We need to get going,' he growls, nodding at the two prostrate figures. 'Wait outside while I see to these two.'

They push back through the low doorway into the dead end street. Something even weird about the weather, Ruby thinks, her head still full of Jin's hands flashing in the air, his virtual transformation into that striking snake, the eagle dropping on its prey.

'The rain's stopped,' Charlie says, looking up, forehead wrinkling, then glancing back at the gate.

Ruby isn't listening to him. She's straining to hear any sounds from inside that hard, rammed earth courtyard. It reminds her of the places she saw near Hankow, when they all went on long outings into the countryside to picnic. More like a village dwelling than something right here in the city of bright neon and swanky hotels.

'What do you think he's doing to them?'

Charlie shrugs. 'I don't care.' But he shifts uncomfortably as he says it, glancing back.

Not the slightest sound to be heard now from behind the elaborately carved door. A string of big characters are chiselled into the green wood amongst carved leaves and tree branches, really complex old forms that are hard to read, but feel familiar. One says *mountain*. One of them has the radical for *dog* in it . . .

That's the trouble with Chinese characters, Ruby thinks, especially the older forms. They always look familiar, but it's like a face rushing past in a crowd, leaving you with a feeling that you should recognise them but don't. She traces a finger on the cold wood,

224

but then the thought is interrupted by a grunt, the sound of something heavy dropping on the ground.

She looks back at Charlie. 'He won't kill them will he?'

'No idea,' Charlie says tight lipped. 'But did you see what he did? Do you think it's some kind of trick?'

'No, Charlie. It was real,' Ruby says firmly. There's something unsettling about Jin, but there's no doubting now that he's some kind of very advanced Taoist master. Like someone who has stepped right out of the pages of *Outlaws of the Marsh* or *Monkey*. What he's doing messing around pretending to be a watchman is anyone's guess, but I saw and felt that *ch'i*, she thinks. It's like he plugs into some kind of electric current that flows up out of the earth and through him . . .

Silently Jin has joined her, the Fedora shadowing his eyes. But they glint there in the depths.

'Let's get back to the temple,' he says brusquely. 'Get you two dry and warm.'

'What about them?'

'Trussed like chickens.'

'You didn't . . . kill them then?'

'What do you take me for? Not in cold blood,' he says, a roguish smile darting across his face.

It's only as he moves away, leading them down the

street, that Ruby realises how drenched she is from that brief but heavy shower in the courtyard. And that Lao Jin's hat and jacket are as dry as a sun bleached bone.

第二十三章

TRAITOR

The rogue shower seems to have passed, and the city is warming to its usual mid-September temperature, the air like tepid bath water as they make their way back towards the river.

Charlie has tried to ask Jin a string of questions about what he's doing here, what link he has to his old man, what Ruby's dad is up to, but Jin has brushed each of them aside.

'But what about Fei?' Charlie persists. 'Why did you think she'd be at Auntie's place?'

'Because I saw her and told her to go there,' Jin says, eyes switching across the busy streets for any sign of threat. 'Unfortunately I couldn't be in two places at once. Not even I can do that. I had to keep an eye out for Ruby too. Green Hand must have nabbed her on the way.'

'So where are we going?' Ruby chips in.

'Back to White Cloud.'

'Won't Moonface go there? And that's the last place we'll find Fei,' Charlie says.

'The Green Hand will be too busy to worry about the temple today.'

'Why?'

'Because they're planning something big. Either today – or tomorrow. Let me focus.'

Jin's silver grey eyes are working hard, peering left and right like a hunter stalking prey as trams bundle past and rickshaw wheels hum the air. At the corner of Nanking and Szechuan Roads he suddenly stalls, body tense, alert, and sweeps them all into the doorway of a seedy looking building. Ruby pulls a face, eyeing the grubby awning above them, proclaiming: PHEASANT HOUSE. ROOMS AND DRINKS. Two foreign sailors are slumped under it, beer bottles still clutched in unconscious hands.

But Jin's eyes are on the road, and Ruby follows his gaze back as three cars come cruising towards them. The sun falls on the gleaming bonnets, rickshaws scurrying away, a Sikh policeman changing his mind as he goes to stop them, waving them quickly on. The running boards of the cars each carry three or four bare headed bodyguards, hard eyes raking the pavements, some with pistols drawn. They're all lean and wiry these low ranking ones who don't wear the hats, their shadows on the street just thin smudges as if there's not enough of them to block the sun. The cars seem to be slowing as they draw near.

Are they looking for us? Ruby wonders, shrinking back into the stinky stairwell, wishing she still had the skullcap to jam down over her blonde hair. One tiring rickshaw man is just a fraction too slow and the first car clips his wheel, flipping the whole thing over.

'Don't worry,' Jin murmurs. 'They won't see us in here.'

As if on a signal the black limos pick up speed, accelerating away through the parting traffic, the thin, bone headed men on the running boards grabbing tight. And then they're gone, powering away towards the Bund, the river and its teeming piers.

'Was Moonface in there?' Charlie whispers, squinting through the one good lens he has left.

For once Jin looks unsure. He pauses, scrunching his face as he stares after the convoy. 'No. No he wasn't. But that *was* his car.'

Ruby, quietly, has been terrified she will see Dad tucked on a back seat. Now, it's as if Jin reads her thoughts: 'And no sign of your dad either. Maybe they've gone to their other lair – it's tucked away in

Nantao near the river. But it doesn't make sense if they're planning what I think they're planning. The checkpoints will be closed and the city will be locked off. Unless . . .'

His voice sinks to the ground, face still screwed in thought.

'Damn it,' Charlie chokes at last. 'We're no closer to knowing where Fei is.'

Jin cocks his head, listening. Is that distant gunfire Ruby can hear now, pricking the air, somewhere further up the Huangpu maybe?

'I will do everything I can to help you rescue her,' Jin says, setting off down the road at a brisk pace. 'But we need to make sure we all keep safe. I need to show you and your friends one or two things that will help.'

Ruby hurries to catch his long strides. 'Won't they be watching the temple?'

But Jin doesn't seem to be listening. He slaps his forehead as if in realization of something and a smile cracks across his face.

Jin leads them past the American Club, onto Canton Road, moving faster, strides lengthening. You can imagine him walking vast distances across the Interior, Ruby thinks, jogging to keep up. Maybe he even walked here all the way from wherever he got that accent. She wonders what he has seen and heard on the way. His eyes when he searches for hers look so worldly wise, as though there's not much he hasn't seen in his time, both good and very, very bad. But his smile is encouraging, and she feels that pulse in her belly and lower back strengthen again.

When she sees the Huangpu refracting light in a thousand glints and flashes, hears the hoot of tugs and creaking of junk rigging, she feels hope rising again, that old feeling of resilience. It can all be OK with this man helping them. Fei will be found and even all the stuff with Dad explained. And the ghosts are being laid to rest one at a time. Jin can do the talismans when she needs them . . .

Away to her left the grand buildings of the Hong Kong and Shanghai Bank, the Palace Hotel, the Cathay catch the light, and further round the curve of the river you can see Jardines, Sassoon, all the big foreign companies that have staked a patch of China as their own. It's an amazing view, she thinks grudgingly, but the real China lies beyond that – where the Huangpu joins the mighty Yangtze. Turn upriver there and three thousand miles of plains and patchwork fields and gorges and old pagodas and teahouses await. So much she wants to see . . .

But now it's haunted by bandits and self-proclaimed

warlords and their armies. At the North Station last year she saw one of their armoured trains roll in to a far platform like some clanking dinosaur, dusty, bullet pocked, blackened by a firefight up the line.

Jin keeps up his relentless pace, turning right along the waterfront past coolies barrowing loads in and out of shadowed holds, their repetitive songs hypnotic. Charlie is lagging a bit behind and she hangs back to let him draw alongside. His face looks drawn again.

'Are you doing OK? *Ni hao ma?*'

He shakes his head. 'I don't know what's happening, Ruby. I'm so worried about Fei. I promised Dad I'd keep her safe. And I'm worried about him and . . .' he stops, reaching up to put his hand to his forehead, looking lost.

'And what?'

'I – well, it's really silly. Really silly. But, back there, when we were running from the Green Hand men, I—' He shakes his head again.

'What?!'

Charlie closes his eyes. 'I'm going crazy too. I saw Tom. Running in front of us. It was almost like he was showing us the way. I'm sorry, but—'

Relief floods through Ruby, a great weight lifting as he says those words.

'But nothing. I've seen him a couple of times.'

'But – but it can't be real, can it?'

'You saw him.'

'Maybe I'm just exhausted or something.'

'We saw him,' Ruby says quietly, wanting to hug Charlie, but holding back. 'He helped us and we're still alive.'

'But it's mad.'

'Mad things happen. Remember what your dad said about seeing your mum?' Ruby smiles. 'Remember when that new building near the Shanghai Club sunk into the ground? Remember the electric girl in the Great World?'

Charlie takes a deep breath.

'I still can't believe it.'

'Then that's fine. Just know you saw it.'

Jin has doubled back, his eyes bright again, impatient now to get on.

'Save it for the temple, friends. We need to get to ground.'

Andrei steps from the Main Hall to greet them as they hurry across the courtyard. He looks from Jin to Charlie and then to Ruby. There's something in his left hand but he shoves it away in his pocket as he comes down the steps, his face clouded with concern.

'I waiting hours for you. Really worry. Where you been?'

'Looking for Fei,' Charlie says. 'Any sign here?'

Andrei runs a hand across his close cropped hair, glancing at Jin again.

'You need talk to Yu Lan. Right now.'

'Why?' Charlie says impatiently, but Andrei ignores him and turns to Jin.

'How can we trust you?'

'How do you trust anyone?' Jin replies levelly. 'Judge a man or a woman by their actions, I reckon.'

'My brother say that,' Andrei snorts. 'He get all way here across Russia and Siberia and look after me and Mama and a man he trust kill him like dog in the end.'

'It's a complicated world, young man. Never just black and white—' Jin says, but Charlie cuts him short.

'What's this about Yu Lan?'

Andrei jerks his head back into the gloom of the hall. 'Just ask him.'

Without another word Charlie hurdles the shaky steps and disappears into the temple. Ruby moves to follow, but Jin holds out a hand, blocking her.

'Just give him a minute, Ruby. Or rather, take a deep breath and don't rush to judgement. On anyone . . .'

But she pushes past, up the two steps and into the

familiar smell of the damp and rot of White Cloud. Her nerves are jangling again, the look on Andrei's face disturbing . . .

Yu Lan's standing under the shadowy figure of the Jade Emperor, the blue and pearl clouds scrolling above. His wiry black hair is standing up as he scratches at it, his pudgy face solemn as he stutters machine gun-like Chinese at Charlie. So fast that even Ruby has a job to understand it.

'. . . and that's the last I saw of her. I tried to find you at your house, and then came back here again and found Andrei.'

Charlie grunts, his hands clenching. He looks round wildly at Ruby, but almost as if he doesn't see her.

'You might have been followed,' he says, turning back to Yu. 'The Green Hand have been watching our place.'

Yu smiles proudly. 'I thought of that. I went home and got an earful from my tutor. They sent me to my room and I shimmied out of the window into a peach tree. Climbed over the back wall. And here I am.'

Charlie's staring at Ruby now, biting his lip so hard it's going white.

'What is it? Is it about Fei?'

He nods. 'The Green Hand have her. Moonface has got her and she's been taken away somewhere. They're

trying to pull Dad out of hiding, she's the bait . . .'
His voice falters, emotion choking him short, but
there's more, she thinks. He's holding something back.

'What is it?' Ruby says flatly. But she's already
guessed the worst.

'Your old man's in it up to his neck,' Yu Lan chips
in when Charlie doesn't answer. 'I was looking for you
earlier and I saw Fei and him coming out of the lobby
of the Mansions. They went towards the river and I
saw them get into the back seat of a big car. It shot off
towards Nantao.'

Ruby's knees go weak, as if the ground has lurched
beneath her.

'Dad and Fei? You're absolutely sure? Maybe he was
taking her somewhere safe . . .'

But she knows that's wrong even as she says it. She
remembers Dad at the front door, arguing with that
thin-voiced Chinese man. '*I don't know where she is,*'
he had said. They must have been after Fei already.
And then that beaten down, defeated look as he
climbed the steps heavily to Moonface's office this
morning. Yu's right, she thinks with a groan. He's
betrayed Fei to the enemy.

'Charlie, I—'

'Not now,' he snaps, his face distraught, and then
stalks away back to the courtyard.

Yu is looking at her. 'Ruby, I'm sorry, but I had to tell Charlie what I saw. Moonface is cunning. My father says he has a way of making people do things. They'll have your dad in some bind he can't escape in any way but this . . .'

Ruby follows Charlie with her eyes, only half listening to Yu as he counts off points one by one, her world crumbling.

'My father says Moonface is cooking something awful up. He's got people on the Council under his control and he's cutting some deal with the Nationalists before they reach the city. Enough people want business to continue as usual that they'll all join forces against the Communists. And Mister Tang it seems is one of *them*.'

'He's not *one of them*,' Ruby shoots back. 'He's Charlie and Fei's dad!'

'Maybe,' Yu says. 'But the Communists have done some bad things themselves I heard—'

'I don't care,' Ruby snaps. 'The main thing is we have to save Fei. Nothing else matters now. Nothing. Not Dad, not the Communists, not gossip and stuff like that.'

Jin brushes past, casting her a quick look as he walks towards the altar, pulling attention with him. He claps his hands and bows low one, two, three times before it.

Then he pulls a matchbox from his jacket, strikes a flame and sets about lighting the candles. He clears his throat of phlegm and his voice, when it comes at last, is richer and deeper than Ruby's heard it before, more commanding.

'We are going to rescue Fei. But it will be a dangerous journey. Although we're all born as brothers and sisters, I'm sorry to say that someone is going to betray us before the sun comes up—'

'Do you mean Dad,' Ruby asks quietly.

'Let's not rush in our judgement. People make a lot of mistakes that way. Don't judge others and *don't* judge yourselves too quickly. There is a long, long way to go for some of us. And for some, death is close by, waiting . . .'

If any of the gang's attention was wavering even a little bit, he has them riveted now.

'But I've seen enough to know that some of you have what it takes. Fei will be saved. Moonface will be beaten.'

Seven candles are burning now and he arranges them carefully to form the pattern of the Dipper, dramatically lighting his face like one of the strange, exotic figures of Chinese opera, features exaggerated as his face cycles through fear and hope and fierce determination.

'Work with the Way and not against it. The Tao Te Ching says: *Where armies fight the nettles soon grow. Force is followed by loss of strength.* Therefore find the right path like water finds the river. Trust what you have within and move within the present moment.'

Silence falls.

And this time it is a long and profound one as Jin's words hang in the gloom. Ruby's eyes drift with the smoke from the candles, up into the rafters where the red and white dragons are fighting their perpetual battle. It's more the tone of Jin's voice that has gripped, rather than what he has said. Life seemed to be falling apart, she thinks. First Tom died, then the ghosts in the Mansions, then that appalling moment in Nantao. Mum going to bits again, and now Dad messed up with the Green Hand . . . but that voice is somehow so familiar. Like I've always known it, she thinks. It's helped me, like I was wandering around in a daze and then I found my way back.

She feels a hand on her shoulder and turns to look into Jin's mercurial eyes.

'Your dad's doing his best,' he says. 'That's all we can do Ruby, make the best choices we can and hope we make enough good ones in a lifetime.'

'How about you?' she asks. 'Did you ever make bad choices?'

Jin sighs. 'A hell of a lot. But when you've been around as long as I have, you get better at it – and you get to make amends for some of the worse ones you have made.'

Charlie has come over to join them, his face grim and set.

'OK, Mister Jin. I'll trust you. I saw what you did to those Green Hand. But let's hurry.'

He holds out his hand. 'I'm ready.'

Ruby puts her hand on top of his, determination rekindled. 'So am I,' she says, glad of the contact.

Andrei hesitates a fraction, and then rests his hand on the pile.

Yu Lan shuffles over, his gown rustling, his face anxious. 'I've only just joined, but . . .'

Jin looks at the stack of hands and nods, before ever so lightly laying his right on top of the rest. 'Good. Now I need you to listen very carefully so I can protect you all from harm.'

'From the Green Hand?' Charlie asks.

'From them, yes,' Jin says. 'And from some rather unpleasant and dangerous spirits.'

第二十四章

AGENTS PROVOCATEURS

Whether it's out of a sense of showmanship – or a ruse to get them all to lay bare what needs to be said – after Jin's ushered them into his cramped cell, he leaves them for a while. 'I just need to see to a few urgent matters,' he says. 'Straw will keep you company.'

The pale dog sidles in past him, glancing up.

'He'll bark if he hears anyone creeping up on us. Won't you, Little Brother?'

The dog slumps down and yawns before setting about chewing at a paw, and Jin slips away.

The gang exchange glances, each clearly wanting to ask questions of the others, but an awkwardness is tangible in the smoky dark. Charlie is the first to speak, impatience pushing out the words. 'What's he up to now? We need to rescue Fei and not mess about—'

'What about you seeing Tom?' Ruby says, cutting

across him. 'You said you saw him yourself.'

Charlie opens his mouth, but then shuts it again and shrugs. Andrei's frustration at struggling to follow the Chinese prompts him to check he's understood. 'What? You see *Tom*? What you mean?'

Yu Lan frowns. 'This is your brother? The one who died?'

Ruby nods, looking anxiously back to Charlie. What has the news about Dad done to his opinion of her family? Of *her*.

'Are you sure you didn't know about any of this, Ruby? With your dad and Fei?'

'How could you think that? Cross my heart, Charlie. And hope to die. I'm as furious with Dad as you are.'

Andrei is waving his hands in the air, trying to get them to slow down. 'Shut up. Listen. I need to know what *your* dad was doing Charlie.'

Charlie looks around at the others, judging the mood. 'None of your business.'

'No secrets between us,' Ruby prompts.

'He's just been doing some printing for the Communists,' Charlie sighs. 'He thinks they have a good point or two and he wants to help them. That's all.'

Andrei screws up his mouth, considering. 'And

what about this man?' he adds, nodding in the direction that Jin took.

'I'm sure we can trust him,' Ruby says.

'One way know for sure.' Andrei says, jumping to his feet and going over to Jin's pack. 'Let's look at stuff.'

'You can't do that,' Yu Lan says.

'Be quiet,' Andrei growls. 'You are new kid. We've been together ages.'

Charlie gets to his feet. 'For that matter we only have your word about Fei, Yu. Maybe we shouldn't trust the likes of *you*. It could be a trap to get me and Ruby.'

Andrei's already pulling items from Jin's battered old pack, rummaging down and pulling out an old sweater, a scarf, some motorcycle goggles, a slim book. The cover is block printed in Russian. Andrei frowns at it, and tosses it onto the bed.

Yu Lan is on his feet now. 'I came here to help you lot. If you don't want my help then you can stick it—'

'Stop it!' Ruby snaps. 'Stop arguing. We're going to do this together. And we're going to trust Jin. And that's THAT!'

As she shouts the last word Andrei straightens up. There's a quizzical look on his face and he takes the object he's just found and moves it into the light of the kerosene lamp.

Ruby's breath catches: it's the spirit bottle, or one very like it – sky blue, dimpled with bumps like the gooseflesh that's been stippling her arms, just the same size, with a stopper bunged down tight inside.

Andrei turns it in his hands. 'Isn't this like the . . .'

'. . . spirit bottle?' Jin completes his sentence, stepping back down into the cell, wiping his hands on the back of his grubby jacket. 'You'll never guess where I found that!'

Ruby frowns at him. 'It looks like something of ours . . .' she says, perplexed, glancing uncertainly at the bottle as if it's a hand grenade with its pin pulled.

'It's the one,' Yu Lan whispers, peering at the label. 'That's my calligraphy on the binding charm.'

They all turn to look at Jin as he takes it from Andrei, and calmly sets about repacking his belongings as if nothing has happened, his back to them.

Ruby's arms and legs have started fizzing like crazy again. 'How did you get that? We threw that down the well so it was gone for good.'

'Oh, it was you, was it?' Jin says turning round, his face solemn. 'Not that easy to chuck things away sometimes. Out of sight is not always out of mind.'

'But how did it get back up here?' Ruby presses. 'Answer me.'

Jin lifts the bottle up to the light, peering through its thick glass. Is that smoke still crouched in there? Ruby thinks, edging closer. Without warning Jin grasps the stopper and, face contracting with effort, jerks it from the bottle's neck. It comes out with a pop.

'No!' Ruby gasps.

But nothing happens. Jin raises the bottle to his flaring nostrils and gives it a tentative sniff. 'Hair tonic?' he asks quizzically. 'Aftershave? Or poison?'

He's teasing, she can tell that and frustration boils over. 'No! That's what we trapped the fox in. We lured him out and trapped him in the bottle and then threw it down the well. Tell me how you have it.'

Lao Jin frowns. 'Foxes aren't easily trapped, Ruby. Maybe you didn't get him in the bottle. Maybe he wanted to be caught.' He looks at Yu. 'Maybe the sealing characters have a couple of strokes in the wrong order . . .'

Yu looks disdainfully back at him, the arrogance back on his round face. 'How dare you. You're just a scruffy beggar. I have respected scholars teaching me—'

'Never mind that now,' Ruby groans, then softens

245

her voice. 'Please, tell me how you got the bottle.'

Jin coughs, a return of that wracking that shakes the phlegm in his chest. He raises a handkerchief to his mouth. In the dim light Ruby thinks she catches a glimpse of red spotting the grubby white cloth.

'Are you OK?'

He nods, recovering his composure. 'I'll be absolutely fine,' he says, looking round the group, his eyes resting briefly on each as if searching for something. 'Just fine. I'll tell you how I got it. I've been here for about five weeks, moving from room to room, most of the summer. I didn't want to disturb you all because you seemed to be having a good time and you didn't need me messing your fun up. But then I realized you were troubled Ruby – and I started to listen carefully. When I saw the watchman's job announced at the homeless shelter the other day I made sure I got it.'

'But we never saw you.'

'You weren't looking in the right places at the right times! It's very quiet here at night and a couple of times I saw you young man,' he nods at Andrei, 'but you didn't see me. You heard things – and so did I. I wasn't making *all* those noises and I tried to work out where they were coming from.'

Jin raises an index finger, then turns it down to

point between his feet. 'The sounds are coming from down there, comrades. Down there under our feet.'

'What – what do you mean?' Ruby whispers, spellbound.

'What I say. Something's moving down there. Something's very restless—'

'You mean like the Black Thing in my room?'

'No. That was mostly in there,' Jin says, pointing at her head, 'I think that was more like your own mind getting confused. Your body and *shen* – your spirit – mixing up all the fear and memories. Lots of people suffer like that.'

Ruby shakes her head. 'What about that American, Woods?'

'Moonface.'

'I told you,' Charlie says.

'So what down there?' Andrei interrupts.

'Things moving,' Jin says quickly. 'I heard a lot of groaning and shuffling down there that night after you chucked the fox down the well and I went to look—'

'Like what?' Ruby asks.

Jin gives a snort. 'Funny thing is that when you get down deep enough there's a ladder set into the brickwork on the wall. It's a deep well, but it's shored up all the way – and here's the thing, when you get to the bottom it's dry. Well, dry-ish. You normally find a lot of rubbish at the bottom of disused wells, dead animals, all kinds of things. But this one's been cleared up a bit, and there's a stream that runs away towards the river. But the water's gone and the tunnel is propped up.'

'So what was making the noise?' Ruby says, wide eyed and pale.

Jin shakes his head. 'Couldn't see. But my guess is Moonface's special fighters. And I found this,' he taps the bottle again, 'just sitting there in the mud.'

'And you didn't see the fox?'

'No. But I could smell him.'

Charlie scowls. 'What do you mean: special fighters?'

'Moonface's best men,' Jin says. 'Shadow Warriors. As real as you and me, Charlie, but they're spirits from the Otherworld. Very dangerous. And I need to teach you how to fight them.'

There's a sound then, before Ruby or Charlie can come back at him. It's distant, felt more than heard like one of the earth tremors that occasionally shake the city. Jin looks up sharply.

'They've started earlier than I thought,' he says. 'Come and have a look.'

He leads them through the crumbling temple, out into the milky sunlight just as another, more distinct rumble, sounds from the direction of Soochow Creek. It's quickly followed by another, but this time from behind, deep in the French Concession somewhere, maybe out towards Boundary Road. Another.

'What's going on?' Ruby asks.

'The city is changing again,' Jin growls. 'Looks like some of the Communists are making a move. Before the Nationalists arrive.'

'But that's impossible,' Charlie says, 'Dad was telling me nothing would happen until just after New Year—'

He cuts himself short.

Andrei and Yu Lan look at him sharply, but Jin holds up his hand. 'I know. I have that information too. Come and have a look . . .'

He leads them to the back of the main hall.

A long wooden ladder is propped there, leaning against the edge of the roof, and he hurries up this now, hands and feet working like a monkey, onto the tiles before the others have even started. It wobbles and shakes as he goes, but it never looks for a moment as if he will fall. Ruby scrambles to follow, grasping the rough wood, pulling herself up, ignoring the growing drop to the cobbles below, eager to keep pace and show she is strong – and trusting him. But what does he mean by Shadow Warriors? How does that link to

Moonface? Jin is crouching at the roof's lip, leaning over, offering her a strong, toughened hand.

'Up you come. Let's take a look at your city, Ruby.'

Sure-footed, he strides up the curve of the rattling tiles, up and up as the roof steepens to the ridge and the sinuous forms of the dragons scroll against the sky. He stands there calmly, one foot planted either side, surveying the scene as the others scrabble up behind, Andrei first, then Charlie. Yu Lan is last, picking his way, hampered by the gown. He holds precariously at the top of the ladder, his eyes flicking away from the others to the drop below.

Jin sweeps his arm across the scene. To their right you can see chunks of the Huangpu flowing behind the mighty buildings of the Bund, and on all other sides the city stretches towards the horizon, countless alleyway houses and narrow streets, the great thoroughfares, the points of the Great World and New World's towers. You can see the North Station through a gap between buildings and a dirty white cloud of smoke is climbing slowly there, rolling on itself. Another rumble shakes the air and a second smoky column starts to lift.

Jin taps Ruby's shoulder. Carefully, one hand grasping a dragon, she turns and sees three or four more puffs of smoke from the French Concession.

And then the distant rattle of what can only be machine-gun fire. Maybe coming from Nantao and the old city, but it's hard to tell as the echoes bounce off the buildings, the water, the factories in Pudong.

Charlie gasps. Not very far away, from a rooftop on the border of the French Concession and the Chinese City, there's a red flag fluttering in the breeze, still being hoisted jerkily up a flag pole. A factory hooter sounds, then another, and a second scrap of red is raised on a building near the barricade.

'But it doesn't make sense. It can't be happening now,' Charlie says.

Jin stares at him levelly. 'I said *it looks* like the Communists are rising up. *Looks*. This is the work of agents provocateurs, Moonface's men disguised as reds letting off smoke bombs and firing a few shots in the air. A trap.'

Away towards the barriers Ruby can hear police whistles shrill on the air.

'They'll be closing the checkpoints already,' Jin says. 'And my guess is Fei and Mister Tang are in the Nantao side. The warlord will get any Communists who show their faces there. And here in the Settlement it'll be Moonface's men – or the authorities arresting them and then chucking them over the barriers and abandoning them to their fate that side.'

'Then we've got to go NOW,' Charlie shouts. 'Get across before it's all shut down or there's a curfew.'

Out on the river a British warship is manoeuvring off its berth, chugging up black coal smoke and sending a bellowing horn into the general chaos.

'I've got a much better idea,' Jin says. 'We can take a short cut and surprise everyone.'

第二十五章

THE GUN

A couple more explosions rattle the city as they clamber down from the roof. What they have seen has shaken Ruby. This is the kind of chaos you expect outside Shanghai. But not here – it's all too much like Hankow. And the rest of the gang seem gripped in their own thoughts as they reassemble in the main hall.

Ruby nudges Charlie.

'Where's Yu?'

'Run home to Papa,' Andrei sneers, glancing at Jin.

'He's going to rat on us,' Charlie says. 'He heard me talking about Dad and the plans and he's going to bring the Green Hand or police here.'

Jin shakes his head. 'Trust me, he's a survivor. He just wants to keep his head down. He wants to inherit what his dad has built.'

'But his sort are part of the problem,' Charlie groans.

'We're all part of the problem,' Jin says.

Ruby's thoughts flick back to her parents, to Amah. She's furious with Dad, but it's hopeless trying to convince herself she doesn't much care right now what happens to him. I still do, she thinks. Of course I do. And maybe all this will tip Mother back into hospital. She thinks of how she gripped her hand on that red-eyed ride back from the mysterious house near Yu Lan's.

Again she has that sensation that Tom isn't far away and she turns to Lao Jin, taking a breath.

'What do you think it means if I saw my brother?'

'That the border between this world and the other one is really thin at times like this,' Lao Jin nods. 'And I reckon that's not the last you've seen of him either. You need him. So he's here and you need to pay attention. All of you,' he adds, raising his voice, 'pay attention! You're going to have to make a dangerous trip, but I can prepare you. I will give you some extra tools to do the job. And then,' he points out into the courtyard, 'and then you can go down into the well, and take the secret tunnel that Moonface and his men have been shoring up. It runs under the waste ground, straight as an arrow as far as I can tell towards Nantao. Right into his lair.'

Ruby's stomach gives a horrid lurch at the suggestion. Into that well brimming with blackness? Under the ground near all those drifting coffins? Worse than that, she can tell already Jin doesn't intend to come with them.

She puts a hand to her mouth, then steadies herself. 'How do you know?'

'I divined the direction,' Jin says. 'A charmed fire lantern, early this morning . . .'

Ruby nudges Charlie, remembering the bobbing flame moving against the wind. 'We saw it passing over the Wilderness – heading for Nantao.'

'If I'm right Moonface has bought this place so he can move contraband and guns in and out of the Settlement at will. Even when the checkpoints and barbed wire seal this place up tight.'

'Let's go now,' Charlie says, eyes burning behind the damaged spectacles.

Jin shakes his head. 'If you do, you won't make it. Take my help – then go.'

'But aren't you coming with us?' Ruby groans. 'We saw how you can fight. I saw what you can do with *ch'i*.'

'I won't be able to come,' Jin coughs. 'I've been called away. It's urgent.'

'But—'

'You will be just fine, Ruby. You'll get through the tunnel fine. My magic will be with you. In the earth down there, or in Nantao, you'll meet the Shadow Warriors, but I'll give you something to deal with them.'

'This is all crazy,' Charlie mutters, but his eyes are rooted to Jin's every movement.

'Then I'll go alone,' Ruby says, swallowing back the fear that's risen in her throat. 'I'm not afraid.'

'Of course you're afraid,' Jin says. 'You'll have to excuse me now. Sit tight, I just want to go out and try and get a better idea of what's happening.'

An hour later the sound of gunfire is still resounding, single rifle shots mixed amongst the thud of distant explosions. Ruby sits on the veranda, hugging her knees, willing Jin to return as soon as possible. A little way off Andrei sits whittling forcefully at a piece of wood with his pocket knife.

'What are you doing?' she asks, watching him rip the blade across the bared wood.

'Thinking,' he says distractedly. 'My brother used to make me things this way. When I was little . . .'

'What are you making.'

'*Ya ne znayu.* I don't know.'

Across the courtyard Charlie has gone to stand at the lip of the well. It's getting darker, and flashes from the sporadic gunfire make the fading light tremble. He's looking down, as if he can't wait to get started, or is preparing himself for what they're about to do. The thought of climbing down there seems so fanciful for a second, so overwhelming. But it has to be done. She knows that.

Ruby gets up and slowly approaches Charlie, the black mouth of the well.

'I just want to get going,' he says as he hears her footsteps approach. 'Get it over with and save Fei – or whatever we've got coming.'

Ruby holds her breath.

Charlie turns away from the drop. 'What did you make of all that stuff he said about some of us having a long journey, and some of us being close to death?'

So he's scared too. Of course he is, Ruby thinks, relieved to see that his anger about Dad has gone for now, that they can talk.

'I don't know,' Ruby says. 'Mum always repeated that silly English rhyme. *Monday's child is fair of face, Tuesday's child is full of grace, Wednesday's child is full of woe, Thursday's child has far to go.*'

'That's a bit simplistic!' Charlie smiles.

'I was born almost bang on midnight between

Wednesday and Thursday,' Ruby says. 'Mum and Dad always argued about which day I was actually born on. It's a toss-up you see, *full of woe*, or *far to go*.'

'Let's hope you were born a minute past midnight then,' Charlie says.

A crow comes beating across the temple roof, perhaps startled by a new volley of machine-gun fire, it's voice creaking as it flaps into the trees that stand over the watching graves.

Charlie looks down at his feet. 'So what's Saturday's child?'

'Works hard for a living. Why? Is that you?'

He laughs. 'Fei and me. Both of us. And only one of us works hard! See, it doesn't really work!'

Ruby's about to answer and then she sees Jin hurrying from out of the gloom. For once the poise has gone from his actions, and he looks rushed, even a bit flustered.

'Hell of a mess out there,' he says, breaking off to bark another ragged cough. 'I saw a group of men bundled into a truck on the Bund. And there's scores of Green Hand out with white and green ribbons tied round their arms acting like they own the place. We'll have to act fast now. Apparently Mister Tang left the safe house hours ago. He must be intending to give himself up in exchange for Fei.'

'Then let's go,' Charlie shouts, leaping to his feet.

Andrei has dropped his sharpened piece of stick and has come jogging over. 'You are back,' Andrei says. 'I am ready.'

Jin looks at him, holding his gaze for a second or two and then nods.

'First I need to give you a few things to help on the journey ahead.'

He beckons them to follow him back up to the shadowy main hall. As he climbs the steps, he reaches into the folds of his jacket and produces a pair of round spectacles. The thin frames shine in the last of the light, an iridescent sheen to the lenses. 'I found these for you, young man,' he says to Charlie, handing them over. 'You need to see clearly. These will be even better than your old ones.'

He turns to Andrei, as Charlie looks at the glasses in his hands. 'I saw you are handy with a sword.' From under his jacket he pulls a short, stubby blade. It gleams a dull green, the soft copper aged and tarnished. 'This is a real one. Old Taoist spirit sword.'

Ruby leans close, reaching out to run a finger along the cold metal, seeing faded characters running the length, smudged by time and the elements.

'What about me?' she says, vaguely jealous of the fact that this beautiful object is in Andrei's hands not hers. He doesn't seem to appreciate it, she sees, just glancing at it distractedly and then wandering away towards the steps, eyes down. Maybe he's still thinking about his brother . . .

'You, Shanghai Ruby, get this.'

Jin moves a few paces away, taking a low stance, then half closes his eyes, focussing, stilling himself. Slowly he begins to circle his hands in the air in front of him, gathering *ch'i* with each sweep and pulling it in towards his abdomen, the movement getting bigger, faster, all the relaxed power of his body flowing into the motion, his hands blurring, breath snorting from his nostrils as the speed increases and his clothes ruffle and snap. It's mesmerising to watch, but makes Ruby uncomfortable too, the force of the action so great that she wonders how Jin can contain it.

Charlie has tentatively put on the new glasses. He peers though them – and gasps. And then Ruby sees it too: a huge ball of energy materialising in Lao Jin's hands. This time it's as big as a watermelon, growing in intensity until it flares brightly, lighting up his clothes and face, chasing shadows through the temple hall. Jin brings the movement to a halt, the *ch'i* like balled lightning as he raises his hands, compressing so it shines even brighter, and then brings it down with a swift movement onto Ruby's head.

A shock wave passes through her. It rocks her to her feet and seems to bounce up again from the floor, warming and expanding her body. She feels her arms and legs loosen, her chest expand, eyes and head clearing.

Jin smiles, stepping back, watching her reaction – but in the dusky light he looks tired now and as if he's aged, his posture slumped by the effort. 'Not bad for an old beggar like me,' he smiles. 'Now you will be OK in the well. Wherever you go, even in the Otherworld. Trust me.'

'In the Otherworld?' Ruby says quietly. In this moment she feels invincible, ready to vault straight into the well's mouth even and face anything. Anything at all.

'What's it like there?' she whispers.

Jin looks up at the painted dragons warring above his head. 'It's a little different for each person. But the old proverb says if you really want *to know the road ahead, ask those coming back.*'

'From the Otherworld?'

'Some people can't rest when they die, Ruby. They can't let go. Or we can't let them go. Everything should return to the great Tao. And then find new expression in a new life. But some can't.'

'Is that what's happened with Tom?'

Jin nods. 'He's wandering. Between worlds.'

'But *what* is it like?'

'Imagine the whole of China, but ploughed under the earth. People say it's a mirror of this world, beneath ours, with officials and merchants and armies fighting and scholars and peasants just like here. Dark roads and rivers, temples and mountains. One of each for every one up here. Who knows, maybe there's even ghost trains and steamships. Spirit aeroplanes buzzing around in dark clouds!'

He leans forward, eyes glittering. 'But now those worlds are merging, so close to each other they're getting muddled up. And you're going to see it all, Ruby. Because you need to. And with what I've given you all, you can banish any Shadow Warriors to their rest, help release Tom to where he needs to go.'

Charlie has been listening, captivated, but now he steps forward. 'But first we rescue Fei.'

'Don't you see?' Ruby says, 'it's all part of the same thing.'

Jin nods again, and turns away, his face falling into shadow.

Distracted, nobody has been watching Andrei as he walked away and let the spirit sword drop with a clunk to the floorboards.

And nobody has noticed his face grimace as he fished around in the hiding place under the steps and pulled out Dad's black Webley revolver.

Nobody sees him take a breath and screw tight the folded piece of paper from his pocket in his other hand.

But they all see him as he comes back, the gun pointed straight at Charlie, face burning with uncontrolled rage.

第二十六章

INTO THE WELL

'You're all Communists,' Andrei says, his voice trying to hold steady, but wavering like the gun shaking in his hand.

Charlie stares back at him, as baffled as anything. 'Stop messing around, Andrei, we've—'

'It was a *Communist* who killed my brother. How could you be involved with people like that? How could you?' His eyes are fixed on Charlie, blazing.

'Don't be stupid,' Ruby says, surprised how calm and controlled her own voice sounds. Almost as if she expected this, had felt this moment coming. 'Charlie had nothing to do with that.'

'Maybe. Maybe not,' Andrei says, as he cocks the trigger, the black mouth of the gun shivering, and then swings the barrel to point straight at Jin. 'But *he* did!'

Jin stands impassively watching, arms hanging by his sides, his breathing slow and controlled.

Ruby steps towards Andrei, holding out her hand. 'Put it down, Jin has nothing to do with—'

But Andrei fires – or his finger accidentally twitches on the sensitive trigger – and the barrel flashes and rocks back his hand. In that fleeting moment Ruby waits for Jin to react – to flick his hand up like swatting a fly – or leap high in the air, or even catch the bullet between his teeth.

But he doesn't. The shot hits him in the centre of his chest and he groans and spins away, knocked back and down by the force, tumbling to the ground, his face already blank.

As if from a distance, Ruby hears her own voice scream, and rushes to where he lies, her insides churning. There's blood already pooling around Jin, as black as calligraphy ink in the half light. Even as she turns him back over, she knows there's nothing to be done.

She hears Charlie shout and a struggle raging behind her, and looks to see him and Andrei wrestling for the gun. There's another flash and simultaneous bang and a chunk of the red dragon's belly explodes above them, falling in chunks to the floor. Charlie drops his weight then, and the movement catches

Andrei by surprise, wrenching the gun from his hands.

'You've got five seconds to get the hell out of here,' Charlie hisses, hands trembling as he cradles the revolver.

Andrei stares at him hard. Then he slowly reaches down and picks up the paper he's dropped. 'Take a good look at this! I found it on a wall near the North Station!'

He throws the thing at Charlie, snarls something in Russian, then turns and walks away across the courtyard, past the well, the watching graves and bamboo. Charlie lifts the gun, squinting through the new glasses that Jin has given him . . .

. . . takes a breath, his finger resting on the trigger . . .

. . . then lowers it again.

He shuts his eyes and hurls the revolver away into the weeds.

Ruby lets out the breath she's been holding, and turns hurriedly back to Jin, hoping that perhaps she's wrong, that the wound isn't so serious or that his *ch'i* will somehow heal him. But his face is as white as hers now, and there's not a hint of heartbeat or breath or life in his limp and bleeding body.

Tears blur her eyes for the second time today, distorting

Jin's features, the weathered face, the silver-flecked hair. His face is very calm and still, but she knows it won't move again. One minute he was brimming with life and *ch'i* and now . . .

She senses Charlie coming to stand beside her, feels his hand on her shoulder.

'He's dead,' she says quietly, eyes smarting. 'Has Andrei gone?'

'For now. But he might be back with the police – or worse.'

'Jin said someone might betray us. If he knew, then why didn't he stop him? Or react?' Ruby groans.

'Maybe he couldn't,' Charlie says quietly. 'Or didn't know who it was. I dunno.'

'But why kill him?'

Charlie holds up the paper he has unfurled to show the picture of a man's face, a crude drawing, but one she recognizes at once: Lao Jin. And above in Chinese the words 'WANTED. DEAD or ALIVE' and below 'MURDERER, ASSASSIN AND COMMUNIST. REWARD OFFERED.'

'It's him, isn't it?' Charlie says. 'Here they call him Hu Jin – but it's him, I'm sure.'

'Murderer,' Ruby whispers. 'I can't believe that.'

Charlie shakes his head, unbelieving. 'Andrei must think Jin killed his brother. Or was involved. No idea where he got a gun from though.'

'It's Dad's,' Ruby says, her spirits slumping even further. 'I brought it here. Don't even know why I did it . . .'

'It's almost like it was meant to happen,' Charlie says, peering through the new lenses. 'Didn't you feel that?'

'Kind of.'

Charlie gazes at the dead man. 'It was amazing that *ch'i* stuff. You were right, Ruby – maybe he was the real deal.' His breath catches and he turns away. 'Didn't save him in the end.'

Ruby gets to her feet. Inside it feels like there's an almighty struggle going on: desperation and shock at what has just happened to this extraordinary friend, but still the power and strength of the energy he gave her bounding along her veins and arteries. And the energy is winning. 'He meant us to go,' she says decisively. 'He said he wouldn't be able to come and that we could do it.'

She gets to her feet. 'We should find something to cover him. And I'm going to take that sword now Andrei's gone.'

Charlie follows her gaze to where the the blade is lying discarded on the floor. He squints harder. 'This might sound weird – but I can see it kind of glowing.

I can see something on the blade.'

Ruby walks over and picks it up, turning its light weight in her hands. It feels fragile, the dull copper almost thin enough to bend. What good can it do?

'It's glowing stronger now,' Charlie says. 'Characters. *Embrace Tiger*, it says.'

Ruby frowns. 'I can hardly make anything out.'

Charlie glances back at Jin's body, hesitant, not wanting to rush her, but that urgent goal is pulling him now. Of course his mind is still on Fei. 'How do you feel? I mean—'

'We're going now,' Ruby says. 'Go and get Jin's pack and put the Almanac in it. I'll find some rope or something.'

Her eyes flick to the well. 'We're going to get Fei.'

She keeps her breathing long and controlled, pushing each nagging thought away as she spreads one of Jin's blankets over his body. He looks smaller, already, as if so much of his height and weight was to do with movement rather than actual physical size and strength. Not much taller than Charlie in fact. Where the *ch'i* blazed, now he looks painfully thin and old. She reaches and strokes his eyelids shut, just like she remembers that bearded French doctor doing for Tom. And pushes the emotion down again with a new breath.

Straw has materialised out of the shadows, his tail down and hanging still for once, his head lowered as if he knows what's happened. In the half-lit trees beyond the gravestones, a crow is flapping around restlessly, croaking, and still gunfire rattles away towards Nantao.

'I'm sorry about your friend,' she mutters, wondering if he might talk again, but the dog simply lies down, watching her with steady eyes. Ruby goes over and puts a hand on his ruffled neck. That moment keeps replaying, as if she can still hear the gunshot vibrating in the old timbers of the temple, becoming a part of that background buzz that she has always put down to the traffic on Bubbling Well Road when they lived there, to the generators in the Mansions, to perpetual thunder or distant goods trains. Maybe the city just soaks it all up and then when it's quieter you can hear it vibrating there—

'Ruby? Ruby!' Charlie is standing by her, Jin's pack in one hand and a puzzled look on his face. 'I found something weird with the Almanac.'

He raises his other hand and the last of the evening light falls on the object clasped there. A tin, clockwork monkey, brass cymbals glinting.

Ruby feels the shivers flying again.

'It's Tom's,' she says, frowning, and takes it from Charlie. The flared butterfly wings of the wind-up key are cold under her fingers, but she gives it a crank or two and then lets go. The monkey bursts into chattering life, clanking its cymbals as frantically as it always did.

At the lip of the well, Ruby pauses and looks back to the temple. Straw has followed them silently, sniffing the air, his tail still clamped between his back legs. Clouds have rolled in, choking what light there is from the sky.

She turns to Charlie. 'Do you think we should go to the police?'

'Don't be daft,' Charlie says. 'They'll be shooting people at the drop of a hat and they won't care about one more Communist getting added to the pile. And they might take me in . . . We need to get going.'

Ruby gives Straw a hug round the neck. 'You better find somewhere safe,' she whispers. At the last minute she has swept up Jin's battered old Fedora and plonked it on her head.

Charlie flashes her a quick grin as he hitches the rope they've found around the well head and drops it into the cool darkness. 'You look like a real hero now. Just like Hu San Niang.'

Ruby looks back at the temple. 'Do you think we'll be back here again?'

'No idea.' Charlie follows her gaze, the fading light

dancing on his new glasses. He reacts then, like he's seen something surprising, and Ruby strains to make out what it is.

But there's nothing except Straw padding back to his friend's body, climbing the veranda steps and lying down next to him in the gloom.

'What is it?'

'Nothing,' Charlie says, taking the glasses off and cleaning them carefully on his sleeve. 'Let's go.'

'Did you see something?'

He pauses – then shakes his head. 'It's too dark to see anything properly. Shall I go first?'

'No. I will.'

If I wait any longer I might lose this courage, she thinks, trying to believe that she's about to drop herself into the well. And into what? She knots her hands around the old rope, swivelling on the ledge of the well, taking a deep breath, then lowers her feet into the mouth, bracing the soles of her shoes against the brickwork, her arms taking her weight. Couldn't ever climb a rope properly in gym, she thinks grimly. Look at me now!

And then she starts to descend.

The frayed hemp bites her hands, but she can feel *ch'i* rising up out of her belly to strengthen her grip, and

272

she edges down, the blackness taking her bit by bit, feet slipping, catching, slipping again on the green and mossy wall. Cool air sighs up past her, rippling her clothes, her skin, rich with the smell of the earth.

With Jin's hat on her head and the spirit sword tucked in her belt she feels she's becoming something new. Not just that she's more like her old self, but something more. Everything that has happened since Hankow has left its mark and changed her: the failure to save Tom, the turn inward as they came home on the British gunboat, the hauntings and fear and jumping at her own shadow. She carries with her the wind chimes and the capture of the fox, the death of Woods and Andrei's treachery and the way Jin fought the gangsters. The way he died.

Life is change.

At least I'm changing, she thinks grimly. But into what?

The mouth of the well is now a small disc, the smell of silty soil filling her nostrils. She swings around, her feet kicking for the ladder Jin described. Nothing yet. Below her the last few feet of rope twists against the shadowed depths.

Nothingness below that.

She edges lower, feeling the shivers come again but accepting them – and her left shin bangs into something sticking from the wall. Quickly she feels for it with a foot and her shoe grips a metal rung. There's another below that – and another. Carefully, she transfers her weight, hands clasping the cold and clammy metal and then she lets go of her lifeline and climbs on down.

And down.

A whispering slithers on the subterranean breeze.

It's like distant water running, or old newspaper shifting in the wind. Or voices maybe, sighing out confused syllables in the depths.

'Wow!' Charlie's voice sounds very small and far away. 'Your sword's glowing like crazy, Ruby.'

She glances down at it, but can see nothing – or is that a very dim light?

'Are you sure?' she calls back.

'Can't you see it?'

'A bit. I think.'

She feels her way on down the ladder, the cool, sweaty rungs under her hands, the disc of light above shrinking, that hissing sound gathering in her ears, chopped by her heartbeat.

How much further? The ground around her gives a low, but distinct rumble, and in her head there's the flash of an image. Coffins moving.

'*Mei wenti*,' she mutters to herself, reaching for the next rung.

And then she feels the squidge of mud beneath the sole of her shoe, and she lowers her weight from the ladder, reaching for the torch in her pocket. When she flicks the switch, she braces for it to illuminate the fox's face, or a Green Hand thug. Or something worse. Anything seems possible now, anything she ever read or heard about, anything she's ever feared.

But there's no one either living or dead to greet her, and instead she sees a subterranean space, a cave of green. It's about the size of a small room, the ceiling arched, the old brickwork crumbling and covered in thick moss and slime. She swings the torch across the dark green surfaces, drops of water caught shining like stars. At her feet the mud sucks at her shoes as she turns, but the well is indeed otherwise dry and following the course of the old stream bed she sees a tunnel running away to her right, in the direction of what must be Nantao, just like Jin said. It's been strengthened, with planks of wood shoring it up, and a thin white wire loops away into it from a reel at her feet, into the pitch black.

She listens hard and hears that shushing sound flowing like a stream around her . . .

'I'm down,' she calls, trying to pitch her voice loud enough for Charlie to hear, but not to disturb anyone. Anything.

As she waits she tentatively flicks the torchlight into the tunnel. The beam falters, a feeble yellow in the thick blackness, the battery weakening. Just damp walls, skeins of green moss and fern and deeper dark beyond. Despite the *ch'i* and her sense of renewed determination, it's a relief when Charlie scuffles down the last few feet and drops to the ground beside her.

'Take a look,' she says.

Charlie blinks, peering through the new glasses at the tunnel, the noodle-like wire sucked into its depths. He whistles softly. 'Just like Jin said.'

'And there's a sound down here, can you hear it?'

Charlie listens for a moment. 'Maybe. Do you think it's the river?'

'I can hear voices in it.'

'Only one way to find out.'

He strides towards the tunnel. 'Let's go as fast as we can. If it starts raining maybe this will flood. There was a drop or two as I climbed in. Put the torch out, it's too bright and it'll tell people we're coming.'

'Then we won't be able to see,' Ruby hisses, hurrying to close the gap. Her goosebumps are really strong now, nudging her freckles, the fine hairs standing on end.

'It's weird,' Charlie says, 'but I can see really well. And your sword's like a beacon anyway.'

276

Even she can see it now. A hint of emerald lightening the blade, the engraved characters in it stoked with spectral light. And you can see that familiar pattern of the stars of the Dipper, repeated again and again.

She brushes past Charlie and enters the low tunnel, ducking her head, feeling the cold, damp air wrap tighter around her.

'I'm going to count our steps,' she says. Good to concentrate on something simple in all this darkness, she thinks, as the roof crouches lower, pressing down.

Fifty paces, a hundred, two hundred, just the sound of their feet in the muck, that static hiss growing around them. It's getting stronger, something like the breaking wave sound you get on the wireless between stations. The white wire loops from hook to hook alongside them, the only sign now of recent activity in the subterranean passageway.

Charlie taps her on the shoulder, reaching out to touch it. 'Maybe it's a phone line or something—'

Above the shushing sound comes a muffled, drawn out moan, cutting him short.

'What's that?' he whispers. 'A ship on the river . . . ?'

'Sounds like it's down here,' Ruby says, looking at the stars glowing on the sword.

'How far does this thing go?' Charlie hisses back. 'We must be well under the Wilderness now.'

'Shhh.'

She listens hard, but the moan isn't repeated, and she pushes on into the soft darkness.

Four hundred, four hundred and fifty, five hundred paces. Ruby's eyes start to ache from the struggle to find any light, but she can see the blade lighting her pale hands and she focuses on that. They must be under the Mansions by now, or very near. The tunnel walls start to widen, shrinking away from them, the roof lifting again so they can stand straight. Some kind of chamber opening up around them, but it's so dark. She reaches for the torch and flicks the beam back into life to reveal a square chamber, much drier, new brick and steel girders at the corners. There are wooden crates stacked to the side, a bundle of rifles leaning against the walls.

Above her a hatch is cut into the roof—

Charlie takes a quick look and then goes to peer into the tunnel where it continues. His breath catches.

'Ruby!'

'What? What is it?'

'There's someone coming. Two. Three maybe . . .'

'What do they look like?'

He swallows hard. You can hear the gulp clearly.

'I think we're in a heap of trouble.'

第二十七章

GHOSTS OF LOST SOLDIERS

The torch beam stutters again and dies.

In the return of the darkness, the copper sword flares, and in its unearthly light Ruby sees figures rushing towards them.

They look like Green Hand men, the stick thin, bare-headed ones, but transformed somehow into something nightmarish as they charge towards them. Their bony fingers are raised into claw-shaped hands, the green flashes on them clear and pulsing livid colour, as if emitting light.

'Look at their eyes,' Charlie hisses.

The figures are dark, but their gaunt faces are each studded with two dull, bloodshot eyes. Like the mad dogs she used to chase away from the family tombs in the countryside when she was small.

'It's them,' she whispers, gripping the sword tighter.

'Like Jin said. Stand back.'

'I've got the gun,' Charlie grunts, rummaging frantically in the pack. 'Picked it up.'

Ruby raises the spirit sword high. *Mei wenti, mei wenti*, she repeats like a mantra, watching the green palms dancing towards her. Mustn't let them touch me, she thinks, instinctively sensing that would mean death.

Charlie straightens, cocking the gun and steadying his hands.

Bang! The muzzle flashes, horribly bright, but the three onrushing shades keep coming. Charlie steadies and pulls the trigger again, the explosion as loud as the first, and one of the wraith-like figures judders to a halt as if it's run into a wall before disappearing before their eyes.

'Got one!' he shouts, but the flash of triumph on his face is cut short as he flies backwards, gripped from behind by something. He lets out a half shout, half scream, the gun discharging wildly again. Ruby feels the bullet carving the cold air, and then *sees* it coming, as if time has slowed again and she feels her hands move, the glowing blade flicking up. With perfect timing it meets the bullet and deflects it away harmlessly into the wall, the copper zinging. And then the Shadow Warriors are on her, dim red eyes cracked with glowing veins, those green flashed palms grabbing for her. She whirls the sword, her feet and arms and legs moving with balance and speed, as if everything is flowing effortlessly from that steady pulse of *ch'i* in her stomach. One of the Warriors jabs bony fingers towards her chest, as if reaching for her heart. She feels her ribs constrict, but with a quick thrust the copper blade goes straight through the thing's belly. She braces for the impact, for blood, but there's no resistance at all. The Warrior goes rigid, its hands flying up as if falling, dissolving in grey-green smoke – and gone. She hesitates a fraction of a second, astonished, then senses intense cold at her back, and sweeps round, blade parallel to the ground, chopping straight through Shadow number two. The red eyes flame and then it too is gone into hissing smoke.

'Ruby!' Charlie screams.

He's on the ground, punching at the thing crouching over him, scrabbling to keep it at arm's length. Ruby takes two fast steps and then leaps clear across the space and slices down, stopping the blow before it hits Charlie. The Shadow shudders, curling up and giving a squeal like a stuck pig – and then she cuts it again and it hisses and disappears.

Wild-eyed, Charlie looks up at her from the muddy floor.

He opens his mouth then closes it again.

'Did you see their eyes?' Ruby asks.

He nods, still speechless.

'Shadow Warriors,' Ruby says, 'Restless spirits . . .'

Charlie shakes his head. 'I saw them. They felt so cold. How the hell did you do that?'

'I don't know. I just let it happen somehow.'

She holds out her hand and grabs his, feeling his palm reassuringly warm and real in hers. Charlie holds her gaze for a long moment.

'Something else, Ruby. Before we climbed into the well.'

'What?'

'I saw Tom again. He was playing with the wind-up monkey next to Jin's body.'

She pulls him to his feet, the image strengthening her even more.

'Do you think we're going crazy?'

'No,' she says. 'And we don't have time to worry about it anyway even if we are.'

She thumps the torch and another feeble bit of light spills across the packing crates. Printed on each in Chinese Characters and English are the words; MUTUAL LOAN SOCIETY.

Charlie wrenches the lid off one of them and whistles darkly, the torchlight picking out sticks of dynamite, coils of wire.

'Moonface hasn't even started yet. There's enough here to blow up half of Shanghai.'

Ruby looks away into the tunnel. 'Then we need to stop him, before—'

She cuts herself short. Distantly, but visible as if lit by dawn light, she can see Tom again. Running away from them, running in earnest, round a bend in the passage, and gone.

They move on quickly, hurrying through the tunnel as it tightens back around them. That whispering rush of sound has died to a soft background pulse. No further sign of Tom, but the urgency of his departure down the tunnel has put fresh speed into their legs.

Ruby's stopped counting her paces, but it must be easily another three or four hundred further on when they hear new sounds coming from the walls, or ceiling of the tunnel. A grinding rumble that you can feel as much as hear.

'That's coming from up there,' Charlie says. 'Tanks maybe?'

Ruby frowns. 'We could still be under the Concession. But we must be very close to the barrier.'

Apart from a few gentle curves the passage has been reasonably straight, gently rising all the time, a trickle of water here and there and a rising note of sewage and brine. The ground's definitely getting wetter, and when she looks down she sees little rivulets snaking between her feet. And then the last of the torch battery is gone.

'Must be raining harder,' she says. 'Perhaps we should get out of here.'

The water is coming a bit stronger, a distinct stream in the bed of the tunnel now, but another fifty paces further it bends sharp right and there's a dim light lifting the gloom. Ruby glances at the sword to see that it's almost extinguished, the copper looking dull and old. Will it flicker every time? she wonders, like a warning. She glances at the gun grasped in Charlie's slim hand.

'Do you know what you're doing with that?'

'Not exactly,' he says. 'Dad always taught us the pen beats the sword. In the end.'

'Where do you think we are?

'Don't know. But let's take a look.'

They edge round the corner to find a hurricane lantern burning. The stream bed runs past a kind of brick landing and climbs away into a low arched tunnel. A fresh surge of water comes out of it, running foul and stinking towards them and wetting their shoes and socks, and with relief they climb up onto the raised platform. It's like a small riverside jetty and from it a flight of rough stone steps leads to a door high above them. The air is tinged now with a new scent – something above the drain smell. Possibly smoke, and the tang of sizzling onions and ginger too?

Charlie looks at the lantern. 'Ghosts don't need lanterns, right? We could wait and see who comes back for it?'

Ruby shakes her head. 'No. Tom was running fast. Like we've got to get a move on . . .'

She grips the sword and climbs the steps to the barred, wooden door, beckoning him to follow.

'If it's real you try and shoot it,' she says. 'And if it's a Shadow leave it to me—'

Before the words are fully out of her mouth, an explosion shakes the wooden door, its flash searing the edges of the frame. There are shouts, some muffled, ragged and gruesome. Like the Consul's wife screamed when the car caught fire in the Hankow riot, a sound she's buried away until now. Ruby counts to three, gathering the *ch'i* deep inside, steadying herself, and then pushes hard at the door. It gives way on the second shove, sending her stumbling through and into an inferno.

Flames are filling the room beyond, roiling black smoke choking the air. Are those shadowy figures moving inside? More Shadow Fighters? Or just people struggling to escape the aftermath of the explosion or whatever it was. There's a stench of gunpowder in the air, and the rattle of a firefight somewhere overhead. A man in flame is rolling on the ground trying to put himself out.

Ruby struggles to see through the smoke, eyes stinging, and then – so close it takes the breath from her mouth – Tom is standing right in front of her. He nods, his eyes urgent, and as the shock rolls through her he holds out his hand and reaches for hers. She reaches back, but at the last moment he fades into the smoke and her fingers close on empty air. Very faintly she hears, or thinks she hears him say: follow me, Ruby. *Lai ba. Lai ba.*

'Keep close,' she shouts to Charlie, and then focuses inwardly on the sound of Tom's voice, echoing like he's whispering down a long tube into her ear.

Now you need to go left, Ruby. Hurry. Now right here. Up these stairs. Through a chaos of smoke and flame, past figures bent double and choking, through a door and up a corridor.

'Tom,' she calls. 'Can you hear me?'

Just hurry, Ruby. Hurry. I'm glad to see you.

The passageway jinks left and they come to another

flight of steps. Tom's standing at the top, his pale arm raised, pointing.

I've got to get back on the boat, he says – and disappears.

Charlie's gasping for breath and fresh air as he catches her. 'We must be – right under the old city now. Sounds like fighting here too.'

They climb this new flight of stairs towards fresher, rain-soaked air and hear the gunfire barking and people shouting. And then, over that, over the sound of the rain, a bright clear voice, they know so well.

'Dad! *Baba*, Dad! Help!'

It's Fei. Bellowing at the top of her lungs, voice like a foghorn cutting through everything.

Together Ruby and Charlie charge to the top step, round a corner and into a courtyard, into the middle of a gunfight, and straight into the crouched form of Ruby's dad.

第二十八章

NIGHT BOAT

Mister Harkner looks as astonished to see them as they are to see him. He's crouched behind a low wall under the covered walkway that runs around the yard, his eyes more bright and alive than Ruby's seen them in ages. The transformation is so complete that it takes her a half second to recognize him, and another half to see that the man supported under his left arm is Mister Tang.

Charlie's dad is clutching his belly, blood trickling through his fingers, his eyes fogged with pain and shock.

'Ruby!' Dad shouts. 'What the hell! Get down both of you!'

'Dad! Help!' Fei's voice calls again and Ruby strains to see where it's coming from.

Charlie pushes her to the ground as machine-gun

fire shreds the air over their heads. She braces her fall and looks up to see two other men and a young woman crouched behind Dad and Mister Tang, popping up sporadically to fire back with pistols, an old rifle, red armbands lashed round their sleeves, their faces grim and determined.

Charlie is reaching for his dad, but Ruby can't take in what he's saying. Instead her eyes are fixed on Dad, fumbling clumsily for English. 'How could you? How could you? You – kidnapped Fei!'

'I did not,' he says. 'I changed my mind and tried to get her away. But they caught us anyway . . .' his voice stutters. 'I was trying to protect *our* family, Ruby.'

'Where Fei?' Charlie shouts in English, shaking Dad's shoulder. 'Where is she?'

'Other side of the yard,' Mister Harkner says. 'Moonface has her.'

'Where are we?'

'Near the river. Nantao.'

'How did you find this place?' Ruby says, ducking as another burst of gunfire rattles the tiles above them.

'A man came to see me. Chinaman. Very impressive. I'd never met him before but he knew everything. He took me to some of your dad's friends, Charlie. We got here just in time to save Mister Tang from handing himself over to them . . .'

'Did he have a hat like this?' Ruby asks. 'The Chinaman?'

Dad nods, confused.

The gunfire has stopped, an uneasy silence hanging on the air as Mister Tang seems to recover a bit and props himself up. 'Charlie,' he says in Chinese. 'The bastard's got Fei.'

Charlie crouches next to him. 'Are you OK?'

'It's not serious. I think.'

Cautiously, Ruby raises her head above the wall. Through the smoke and rain you can just make out hazy figures moving.

'Get down, for God's sake,' Dad hisses.

'I can see her!' Charlie shouts. 'I can see her, he's taking her. Fei!!"

'Charlie? Charlie!' a voice answers, and then is cut short.

Ruby squints hard, but obviously Charlie's eyesight is sharper than hers and she can make out nothing but vague shapes. At the last she thinks she sees a small figure struggling in a doorway on the far side, being dragged away by a bulky figure. Yes, it's Fei, twitching her head, the plaits flying. Another volley of firing sends them back down behind the low wall.

Ruby looks back at Dad.

'I'll be back' she says, gripping the spirit blade tighter. Cross my heart.'

'You're going nowhere—'

'Get Mister Tang to safety somewhere. Charlie and I are going to save Fei. I have to do it. Give him the gun back, Charlie. It's no use to us.'

Charlie nods and holds out the Webley to the astonished Mister Harkner.

'Just tell me one thing,' Ruby says quietly. 'Have you seen Tom?'

'Tom?' Dad looks startled, but instead of shouting her down his voice drops to a whisper.

'No. But your mother says she keeps seeing him—'

Charlie's back by their sides. 'We go now,' he says in hesitant English. 'Friends shoot and we go. You help my father.'

If Mister Harkner is going to argue, the volley of shots that rings out from their side of the wall drown his words. Ruby looks into Charlie's eyes, meeting his gaze for a long heartbeat – and then she nods once, and she's up and over the wall, sprinting across the courtyard, towards the doorway on the far side where Moonface dragged Fei. Bullets sting overhead, the rain smacking her face as she hears Dad shouting.

'Rubyyyy! Come back!'

Charlie's close behind as she reaches the doorway

on the other side, and now his voice shouts her name.

'Ruby, look out!'

From out of the smoke a thin dark figure blocks her way, reddened dull eyes, hands glowing green, clawed fingers reaching for her. Another Shadow Warrior, face twisted in a snarl. It scares her more than the ones in the tunnel. That felt right to meet those things down there, but this is the real world, with Dad and Mister Tang and the sound of the doomed uprising all around them. The thing looms over her, hissing a string of Chinese swear words, and then moves like a snake to strike. Again the copper blade leaps in her hands as if jolted with electricity, and again her hands move with the *ch'i* flowing through them, slashing diagonally. But the Shadow sways back and she misses, and then it's right beside her, cold breath flowing on her neck, its fingers jabbing for her head. She feels it snag her hair, but then her reflexes take over, and she ducks just in time, the sword circling and slicing up through its torso. There's a stink of smoke, like burning rubber. And it's gone.

The brief fight has left her breathing hard, and the sword seems to be weighing heavier in her hands. No sign of the glow on its blade as that Shadow came at her.

Fei calls again, but distantly now and Charlie's

running like fury, down the the stone-flagged corridor to a barred gate. It's hanging loose on its hinges and he's already pushing through it as she sets off to follow.

Beyond lies a deserted cobbled alley, the rain slicking the stones. Ruby chases after Charlie, round the next corner and onto a broader street lined with lorries, abandoned barrows and crates, waiting to be looked on to junks.

There they are! Moonface is pulling Fei at speed towards the dark space at the end of the street, the void where the river runs. He has four or five of his henchmen with him – real men by the looks of it, not the Shadow Warriors, Fei fighting in his powerful arms.

'Stop!' Charlie screams. 'Leave her alone.'

Moonface comes to a halt. He turns, features running with rain and the distant flames from the fires lighting the sky.

'She's coming home with me,' he shouts, his voice a growl. He snaps his fingers, a sharp sound like a chicken bone breaking. 'If you follow me you will die.'

'Give her back!'

The gangsters raise their guns and unleash a hail of bullets, sending Ruby and Charlie diving behind the crates. Ricochets sigh and moan around them, pinning them down.

'We can't take them all on,' Ruby groans, peeping through the crack between two tea chests. 'I can't see what's happening.'

Charlie presses his head close to hers, rain running on the lenses of his new glasses.

'They're getting into a motor launch. All of them. Casting off.'

The gunfire has stopped at last, and they hear an engine splutter into life before rising to a throaty roar.

'Come on!' Ruby shouts and bursts from cover, sprinting towards the river, her feet slipping on the cobbles, the sword glowing again and casting a green pallor around them.

But they're too late. As they reach the jetty they're just in time to see the boat's wake curve away on the Huangpu. The motorboat speeds downstream, towards the great buildings of the Bund, the skeletal shape of the Garden Bridge. One of the moored gunships is sweeping the dark river with a searchlight and as it moves across the water they see Fei for a second, starkly lit as she's bundled below deck.

And even more briefly as the launch plunges back into the night, they catch a glimpse of a figure on the stern.

It's a fox, sitting and gazing up at the white moon

that's just briefly appeared in a gap in the clouds. Then it, the launch, Moonface and Fei as good as wink out of existence.

第二十九章

THE WAY TO THE DISTANT MOUNTAIN

Time and the river flow.

The rain keeps falling and slowly seems to quench the gunfire and flames across the city.

'What did he mean about taking her home?' Ruby asks as half an hour later they sit disconsolately in the smoky ruins of the courtyard house. They've been silent for a while: too much to take in. Too many hours without sleep, too many bursts of adrenaline and fear, too many extraordinary things to process and try to understand.

The firefight is over and the place seems deserted. No trace of Dad or Mister Tang, or the young men and woman.

Charlie groans. 'I don't know. But they say his home village is a hell of a long way up the Yangtze. That's his stronghold. Hundreds of miles.'

'But why take her?'

'I don't know.'

'Did you see that fox on the boat?'

He nods.

'What do you think it was doing there?'

'*Bu zhi dao*,' he says in Chinese. Then in English. 'I do not know.'

'So what are we going to do?'

'You should go home.'

'No way. We have to follow them.'

'But how? I'm not even sure how we can get back into the Settlement now.'

Ruby smiles, feels a bit of the strength and courage welling up again. 'The tunnel of course. And then we'll head inland, into the Interior and we'll find her, Charlie.'

'You should go home. Forget about Fei and me.'

She shakes her head. 'No. Way.'

It takes a while to work out how to find the way back to the tunnel. The smoked corridors still smouldering and confused.

At the bottom of the second flight of steps they find the lantern still burning steadily. Charlie picks it up and holds it over the channel below. More water is flowing into the old streambed, but it's only ankle deep, and slowly – tired now – they make their way down the long, soggy trudge through the darkened tunnel. At Ruby's side the spirit sword is dull and lifeless, and they meet nothing but their own thoughts and shadows as they make their way under the earth to the temple.

Ruby keeps hoping for another glimpse of Tom – maybe even of the chance to talk to him, to ask him what it's like in the Otherworld.

But even he seems to have deserted them for now.

A long hour later they find themselves at the bottom of the well and exhaustedly climb the ladder to the rope. It takes all Ruby's remaining strength to drag herself up the rough hemp, and scramble over the crumbling wall, before slumping to the ground in a heap. The rain has stopped, clouds clearing overhead and the moon spilling down again, fraying their departing edges. She takes a long breath of the fresh air and waits for Charlie to join her.

When he does, he takes a moment himself and then clears his throat.

'It'll be really, really dangerous Ruby. The Interior's a complete mess. Warlords and bandits and heaven only knows what—'

'We're going, Charlie.'

'If we go, we might not come back.'

'We're going. Do you know where the village is?'

He sighs. 'No. But we can find out.'

Something moves in the shadows, and the sound of a snapping twig puts them instantly back on alert.

But it's just Straw. He slinks out of the undergrowth, tail wagging, evidently pleased to see them, coming over and licking Ruby's face with his rough tongue, shaggy eyebrows raised as if in greeting, or question. Then he backs away and lifts his head to the moon chasing through the rainclouds – and barks briskly.

He looks back towards the temple, then trots away, across the courtyard, weaving through the weeds and through the gravestones, keeping up that repetitive yap of a bark.

Two syllables over and over and over again. It sounds a bit like *Lao Jin* if you listen carefully.

'You're going to think I'm crazy,' Ruby says cautiously, 'but what if I said I think he can talk?'

Charlie holds up both hands.

'Whatever you say.'

'He wants us to follow. He's saying Jin's name.'

Above them the sky is turning pale, dawn breaking across the city.

They move to where Straw is still giving short, sharp

299

barks, and see he's standing in front of a gravestone. No name on it, no dates, that Ruby can see.

Just a string of Chinese characters: *gone back to the mountain.*

But it's the photograph framed behind glass that reaches out and grabs her attention. It's an image of a young man blurred by condensation. Bending close, her skin prickling again with hundreds, thousands, a million pins and needles, Ruby peers through sudden obliterating tears to see a face she knows well.

The man looks remarkably like Lao Jin. But younger, much younger, seething with vitality and life. But it can't be, can it?

He's staring back solemnly, determinedly from the photograph as if urging her on.

Thursday's child has far to go, she thinks, and her mind floods with the image of a river shining like beaten metal, snaking away under dark and restless clouds into the vast continent behind her.

Old Shanghai . . . is life itself.
So much life . . . so strongly flowing – the
spectacle of it inspires something like terror.

Aldous Huxley, 1926.

Author's note

A reader familiar with Chinese language will spot that I have mixed various methods of writing names and words in Roman letters. Here's why.

Written Chinese developed from simple pictograms like tree 木, moon 月 – to a collection of many thousand ever-more complex characters. Some of these contain clues as to how they are pronounced, some don't. Some are made of just one or two strokes, some of many, many more.

When Westerners met the language they tried to find ways to write characters using the Roman alphabet. Each system had its benefits, but also its problems – and names and words have been written in various different ways over the years as ideas and history changed.

The two main systems (the older, academic *Wade-Giles,* and the modern *Pinyin*) write some very important words in this book differently. What Wade-Giles called the *Tao*, Pinyin writes as *Dao* – (which actually gives a better idea of its pronunciation). Charlie and Fei's surname would be *T'ang* in the older system, and *Tang* in the newer. To further complicate: some place names were known by Westerners by 'Post Office' names. In this system what today is *Beijing* (the modern capital) was romanized as *Peking*.

I have generally opted for place names as they would have been known to Westerners in Shanghai in 1926. Hence *Soochow* Creek, rather than *Suzhou* as it now is. For 'the Way' I have used *Tao*, as still more familiar than *Dao*.

Most other names and snatches of Chinese have been written in Pinyin. For the river flowing through the city I went for the Pinyin *Huangpu* as it causes less sniggering than the older *Whang Poo*.

Fortunately, whilst other places have changed the way they are written – or like *Hankow* even their names – Shanghai has always been *Shanghai*.

Acknowledgements

Some elements of this book have been forming in my mind for many years. Excited as a young boy by TV series such as *The Water Margin* and *Monkey*, I became fascinated with Chinese culture and eventually chose to read Chinese Studies at University. Later I worked on various TV and cinema projects drawing on the history of Shanghai and China. My thanks to everyone who taught or otherwise inspired me over the years.

Specifically for the writing of *Ghosts of Shanghai* I would like to thank my agent Kirsty McLachlan for her constant support, and my editor Jon Appleton for his insight and care. My heartfelt gratitude also to Isabel, Joe and Will who helped road test vital ideas and passages in this first part of Ruby's Otherworldly journey, and upon whose good humour I heavily depend.

Welcome to The Mysterium, a circus with a dark and thrilling secret at its heart . . .

Born and raised in the wild and weird Mysterium, Danny Woo is trained – like his parents before him – in the circus arts of sleight of hand, escapology and hypnotism.

When his mum and dad are killed in a mysterious fire, Danny's world is shattered. But worse – he suspects there's more to the Mysterium than meets the eye.

When an explosion rocks him and his school to their foundations, Danny heads for Hong Kong – and a confrontation with the criminal masterminds of the shadowy Forty Nine.

But can he rescue his kidnapped aunt and make an impossible escape?

MYSTERIUM
THE PALACE OF MEMORY

Danny Woo has survived yet another attempt
on his life – but is no closer to finding out who
killed his parents, and why.

At first, he feels betrayed when he learns that
the Mysterium – the circus he lives and breathes –
has reformed without him. He *has* to join his
friends, but this means getting close to the enemies
who want him dead. Luckily, Sing Sing is back
to help.

But the Forty Nine are never far away. And there's
a deadly new enemy shadowing Danny's
every move . . .

THE WHEEL OF LIFE AND DEATH

The Mysterium are heading to Berlin for the first time since the fire which killed Danny's parents – and changed his life for ever.

But danger lurks on their journey. A mysterious biker is following them. And Danny is troubled – will he and Sing Sing overcome the legacy of their shared past?

Time is running out. As the snow starts to fall, Danny races to decipher Dad's clues and expose Centre – the dark heart of the Mysterium who wants him dead . . .

www.themysterium.net
www.hodderchildrens.co.uk